'STO

ACPL ITEM

DISCARDED

P9-EDO-481

Fiction
Shannon, Jacqueline
I hate my hero

DO NOT REMOVE
CARDS FROM POCKET

92

ALLEN COUNTY PUBLIC LIBRARY

FORT WAYNE, INDIANA 46802

You may return this book to any agency, branch,
or bookmobile of the Allen County Public Library.

DEMCO

I Hate
My Hero

I Hate My Hero

JACQUELINE SHANNON

SIMON & SCHUSTER BOOKS FOR YOUNG READERS
Published by Simon & Schuster
New York   London   Toronto   Sydney   Tokyo   Singapore

Allen County Public Library
900 Webster Street
PO Box 2270
Fort Wayne, IN 46801-2270

SIMON & SCHUSTER BOOKS FOR YOUNG READERS
Simon & Schuster Building, Rockefeller Center
1230 Avenue of the Americas, New York, New York 10020
Copyright © 1992 by Jacqueline Shannon
All rights reserved including the right of reproduction
in whole or in part in any form.
SIMON & SCHUSTER BOOKS FOR YOUNG READERS
is a trademark of Simon & Schuster.
Manufactured in the United States of America

10 9 8 7 6 5 4 3 2 1

Library of Congress Cataloging-in-Publication Data
Shannon, Jacqueline. I hate my hero / by Jacqueline Shannon.
    p.   cm.
    Summary: Although eleven-year-old Rachel is excited
to be working with her best friend Cherry Hill on her
classroom's video news she sees the friendship falling
apart when Cherry Hill saves her from choking and becomes both
a hero and a snob.
    [1. Friendship—Fiction.   2. Heroes—Fiction.
3. Television—Production and direction—Fiction.
4. Journalism—Fiction.   5. Schools—Fiction.]   I. Title.
PZ7.S5288Ih 1992 [Fic]—dc20   92-8909   CIP
ISBN: 0–671–75442–4

For Carleen Hemric
who was, for me, that teacher
every child should have
when the spark first appears

I Hate My Hero

CHAPTER ONE

So many kids wanted to be the anchor kids on *The Room 11 Video News* that Mrs. Desideri decided we'd have to vote on it.

"Now, remember," she said, collecting our wadded-up slips of paper in the black beret Benny McVie always wore to school. "The anchor kids will read the news on camera and hold the broadcast together. So we need a couple of good speakers who are also sharp and quick-witted. This is not a popularity contest. It is not a beauty contest."

Yeah, right. Then you tell me why Marina Dobbs and Cherry Hill Summers were elected.

I snuck a look at Marina, two rows over and one desk up. She was just sitting there wearing her little amused half-smile, as usual, even while about thirty kids called out "Congratulations, Marina!" Every hair on her blond head was perfectly, fluffily in place. It glinted in the sun shining through the window behind her and looked like that angel hair we put around Jesus's manger on top of the TV every Christmas. Marina hid a yawn.

It was a classic Marina Dobbs reaction. She specialized in being aloof and a little mysterious at all times. And strangely enough, that made all the kids at school crazy about her. They'd follow her around like puppies, complimenting her on every single item she was wearing (even her *socks,* for crying out loud) and asking her eight million questions. And about all Marina ever said back was "Yes," "No," or "Oh?" How do I know this? Because for the first couple of months after Marina came to our school last September, I'd been one of those adoring puppies yipping and nipping at her feet.

Marina said her "Oh?" with her head slightly cocked to the left. It looked and sounded very cool, so it spread through John F. Kennedy Elementary School like chicken pox. You heard "Oh?" about eight million times a day.

Cherry Hill Summers was Marina's exact opposite. I don't mean her looks—like Marina, Cherry

Hill was tall and had long blond hair. I mean opposite in personality.

She got her name from the fact that her parents met each other in this town in New Jersey called Cherry Hill. Mrs. Summers had divorced Mr. Summers three years ago, and she and Cherry Hill had moved here to San Diego. Which is about as far away from Cherry Hill, New Jersey, as you can get in America.

Cherry Hill insisted on being called by her full first name—Cherry Hill—and not just Cherry. She could be touchy about things like that. But she was also friendly and could be dramatic in a really amusing way. She was hilariously funny too. So you can understand why she was so popular. Sometimes, she was mean-funny. She'd tell the kind of jokes you feel crummy laughing at but you can't help it. For example, that morning at recess, she'd asked me, "Have you ever seen Stevie Wonder's house?"

"No, why?" I said.

"Neither has he!"

Let's see . . . funny, friendly, touchy. Did I leave anything out? Oh, yes. Cherry Hill Summers was my best friend. She'd been my best friend for two years, since the beginning of fourth grade.

It wasn't until Mrs. Desideri clapped her hands

and started toward the front of the room that I glanced back at Cherry Hill, sure that she'd be beaming with pride and gratitude at being voted anchor kid.

But she was just sitting at her desk wearing a little half-smile.

"I knew you'd win," I heard Benny McVie say to her.

"Oh?" said Cherry Hill, cocking her head to the left.

At first I thought she was just kidding, making fun of Marina. I expected her to burst any second into her usual loud haw-haw-haws that were so contagious. But then Devon Gonzalez said something to her I couldn't hear and the same thing happened.

"Oh?" Cherry Hill said.

I gagged. I really did. I was so surprised. Cherry Hill had been the one person in the entire school who was not impressed by Marina Dobbs. In fact, she couldn't stand Marina. She called her Marina the Mannequin because Marina just stood around being so "oh?" about everything.

Now I tried to get Cherry Hill's attention. I wanted to give her the finger-down-throat gesture about the way she was acting. But she was too busy staring off into space wearing that phony little half-smile of Marina's.

4

"Hey, everybody!" Mrs. Desideri said, clapping her hands again. "I'm going to announce the rest of the assignments for *The Room 11 Video News.* I put a lot of thought into this. After all, we are the first class at Kennedy to ever attempt such a project. So no complaints, please!"

She looked down at the clipboard in her hand. "The camera crew will be Jane Reynolds, Porter Delay, and Annie Bos."

Weather girl, weather girl, weather girl, I said to myself silently. We'd been allowed to submit suggestions to Mrs. Desideri about which jobs we wouldn't mind having, and I'd put down weather girl as my first, second, and third choices.

"Our political commentator will be Casey Chase."

Weather girl, weather girl, weather girl. True, speaking in front of a group had always petrified me. But I figured that the weather girl wouldn't have to say much if anything; she'd just stand in front of the camera in some great-looking outfit and stick a happy-face Mr. Sun on a map of Southern California.

"The news writers will be Betsy Smith, Julie Kooda . . ."

Weather girl, weather girl, weather girl. I squeezed my eyes shut and crossed my fingers. When Mrs. Desideri had posted the list of jobs for *The Room 11*

Video News the week before, Cherry Hill had pointed to "news writers" and said, "All the quiet, brainy types will get stuck doing that." I'd had this kind of sick feeling that Mrs. Desideri would—

" . . . and Rachel Harper."

That, of course, was me.

Everybody knew that the news writers were going to have to do all the work while the anchor kids got all the glory.

Glenn Vandever, the Cutest Boy in the Whole School, who happened to sit one seat up and one seat over from me, turned around. "Better luck next time," he said to me, and then he smiled.

Oh, great, that's all I needed. Glenn Vandever had been smiling at me a lot lately. And the problem was, I could not smile back at him without the corners of my lips shaking and twitching up and down about three feet. He just made me feel so shy and nervous because he was so cute and everything. I did what I usually did when he smiled at me: I pressed my lips together really tight over my braces and hoped that passed as a smile. Yes, I'm sure I ended up looking meaner than a rattlesnake. But I'd already decided that it was better to look like a snake than an idiot. Glenn shrugged and turned back around.

A few minutes later, Cherry Hill and I were on

our way home. She was still acting weird—nodding at people in a very snooty Princess Diana way. It wasn't until we turned the corner onto Stanford Avenue—and there were no other sixth-graders in sight—that she threw her backpack down on the sidewalk, jumped into the air, and slapped my hands in high fives.

"Aw-right! I'm an anchor kid! Move over, Connie Chung!"

Now *that* was more like it.

Cherry Hill picked up her backpack. "Thank you, thank you, *thank you* for your vote, Rach."

I laughed nervously. Actually, even though I knew I'd never win, I'd voted for myself, just so Mrs. Desideri would see that *somebody* thought I was pretty hot. But Cherry Hill just walked on and didn't seem to notice I hadn't said "You're welcome."

"Can you believe Mrs. Desideri appointed David Jenks as the weather person and Felicia Fremont as the sports reporter?" Cherry Hill said. "Just to prove that she's not sexist, I guess. But *Felicia Fremont?* Come on. She's such a lump she's never even been able to run all the way to first base. In fact, I don't think I've ever seen her hit the ball. We're talking about a real sports expert there."

"And David Jenks is so dumb," I said, "he probably thinks a cumulonimbus is a dinosaur."

Cherry Hill laughed. That's the reason we were best friends. We always made each other laugh.

She made like an ape. "Oo-oo-oo. Well . . . uh . . . the sun's shining, which I guess means it's . . . duh? . . . sunny outside right now. And, uh, tonight it'll be real . . . dark!"

I doubled over laughing.

"David Jenks is going to be quite an act," Cherry Hill said. "And all he'll be doing is being himself."

"Speaking of acts," I said, "what was with that Marina Dobbs act you put on after the election?"

"What do you mean?"

"You know what I mean. The little Mona Lisa smile. The thank-you-my-peasant nods. And, of course, the 'Oh?' I kept waiting for you to burst out laughing. And when you didn't, I kept waiting for me to barf."

"Oh?" she said with an exaggerated cock of the head. She was trying to make it all a joke.

But I wasn't going to let her. "Come on, Cherry Hill. I thought you couldn't stand Marina Dobbs. Marina the Mannequin, remember?"

Cherry Hill flicked her hair over her shoulder and turned to me with narrowed eyes. "What does Marina Dobbs have to do with it anyway? Maybe I'm just tired of everybody expecting me to get up and do a cancan or something to entertain them every minute of the day."

"Oh," I said—seriously, with no question mark or cock of the head. But that seemed to make her angrier.

"You're just all bent out of shape because Mrs. Desideri stuck you with being a news writer," she said.

"Am not."

"Are too."

"Am not."

"Are too."

"Not."

"Too."

"Not."

"Too."

"Okay, maybe I am, a little," I said, knowing from experience that she could keep up her side of that kind of battle for hours.

She was immediately my good old loyal best friend Cherry Hill Summers again. "Don't you worry," she said. "The first time David Jenks makes a mistake, I'm going to insist that Mrs. Desideri replace him with you."

"Maybe he'll mispronounce 'clouds,'" I said.

She stole my next line: "'There are lots of clods here today!'"

We ran to my house, laughing.

CHAPTER TWO

We went in through the kitchen door and slapped our hands over our mouths to stifle our groans. Because there, cooling on the counter, lay a freshly baked batch of my mother's dreaded "fiber bars." We ran for the refrigerator, and I grabbed for a plate of some cold homemade pizza . . . but it was too late. My mom appeared in the doorway.

"Oh, good! You're hungry!"

We weren't exactly in a position to deny that.

"Have a fiber bar or two."

Fiber had been my mom's obsession for about the past year. Somehow, she'd gotten the idea that it could prevent everything from heart attacks to ingrown toenails. We were forced to eat some sort of high-fiber food at every meal. If there wasn't any fiber in the meal itself—in the form of, say, broccoli with cheese sauce—we had to eat a fiber bar for dessert. Or a handful of that horrible high-fiber bran cereal that looks and tastes exactly like twigs.

My mom put fiber bars on napkins and set them on the kitchen table. She made them from a recipe that she refused to show anyone. My dad privately swore that was because she secretly put shredded cardboard in those fiber bars. Everybody hated them. But no one had the courage to refuse them. Cherry Hill, at least, tried.

"Those give me gas, Ruthie," she said, wrinkling her nose at them. Everybody called my mom Ruthie. Everybody but her children, that is—me, my ten-year-old brother Cameron, and my thirteen-year-old sister Tina.

"A little gas isn't going to kill you," my mom said to Cherry Hill.

I sighed and dragged a half-gallon of milk from the refrigerator to the table. We'd need it to choke down a bar or two. I sat down, fervently hoping that my mom would leave so we could quietly wrap the fiber bars in a napkin and chuck the package in the trash. No such luck.

She sat down with us at the kitchen table, propping her feet up on a spare chair. She dressed pretty cool for someone her age, probably because she taught college classes every morning. She was wearing black leggings, a neon-pink oversized T-shirt, and a pair of L.A. Gear running shoes.

People were forever telling me, "When you get older, you're going to look exactly like Ruthie." My mom was slender and graceful with short thick hair the same smoky-brown color as mine, and a thin straight nose that was just a teeny bit too long. She wasn't exactly pretty but she could look really chic when she dressed up. So it always used to please me when people said I took after her. Then, right about the time I turned eleven, I realized that my mother was only an inch taller than me. If I was only going to grow one more inch in the next thirty-two years, I'd just as soon take after my dad, who's tall, thank you very much. My dad is on the plump side, but if I had to inherit the possibly-plump gene in order to get the tall one, fine. You can always subtract inches from your hips. You cannot add inches to the top of your head.

"Come on, you two," my mom said after we'd choked down a bar apiece. She smacked fresh bars into our hands. "Go for it. It'll clean out your system. Get ya growing." She glanced at Cherry Hill and chuckled. "On second thought, honey, I think you've done quite enough growing for one year."

Cherry Hill blushed. That's the problem with being a pale blonde, I guess. You can't hide it when you're embarrassed. When Cherry Hill blushed, she looked like a cartoon character who's just had a bucket of red paint dumped over her head.

My mom wasn't implying that Cherry Hill was fat. She was talking about her bustline. Cherry Hill had spent most of the summer at a Colorado dude ranch owned by a friend of her mother. And she'd come back with the figure of an eighteen-year-old.

"What'd they feed you up there—cattle hormones?" my mom asked her, wide-eyed, the first day she was back. "You look like a Barbie doll!"

Now, to me, this would have been a fantastic compliment, since, as we all know, Barbie has BIG ONES.

But Cherry Hill had definitely not been pleased. "I hardly remember what a Barbie doll looks like, since I haven't played with one in ages," she had sniffed. "*Très bébé.*" She'd come back from Colorado with that phrase, and for the first two weeks she'd been home it had been *très bébé* this, and *très bébé* that. It never caught on at school, though. Not like "Oh?" had. I guess kids just felt uncomfortable about *très bébé* because it was foreign.

Foreign and incorrect, by the way. Cherry Hill said another guest at the ranch, a gorgeous French actor named Pierre, had taught her the expression, and that it meant "how very babyish." Cherry Hill didn't know that French had been my mom's minor in college. My mom privately informed me that *très bébé* translated as "very baby."

"So this Pierre is probably a trendy phony," my mom said. "But let's not embarrass Cherry Hill, or spoil her memory of this so-called French actor, by correcting her."

Still, she went dashing from the room whenever Cherry Hill said *très bébé* so that Cherry Hill wouldn't see her laughing.

Now, with her face still red but her eyes twinkling, Cherry Hill stuck her nose into the air. "You should watch what you say to Cherry Hill Summers, Ruthie," she said. "You are looking at the future anchorwoman of the Channel Nine *Eyewitness News*."

We filled my mom in on Cherry Hill's being elected one of the anchor kids of *The Room 11 Video News*.

My mom hid a smile. "Don't tell me you're going to grow up to be one of those blond airheads like Dianna Duvall." Dianna Duvall was the anchorwoman on the Channel 9 *Eyewitness News*.

My mom put on a big, vacant Dianna Duvall smile: "And two people who were hiding from police in a trash can were crushed to death when a garbage truck accidentally picked them up, Stan!"

Cherry Hill fluttered her eyelashes and did her own Dianna Duvall: "What's an airhead, Ruthie?"

My mom got up and swatted at her playfully. "Why don't you guys go in and watch *3-2-1 Contact*?" My mom felt it was her duty to push PBS programs, sort of the same way she felt she had to promote flossing.

"We're too old for *3-2-1 Contact*," I said.

"*Très bébé*," Cherry Hill said with a yawn.

My mom flew out of the room. We heard her burst out laughing in the family room.

Cherry Hill looked at me with her eyebrows raised. "Did we say something funny?"

I shrugged and bit my lip hard to prevent myself from laughing with my mom.

"I just remembered a joke Larry told me," my mom called. Larry was her office mate at the university. They both taught English.

"What was the joke?" Cherry Hill called.

"Never mind. It's . . . um . . . R-rated."

"That's really rather rude, Ruthie!" Cherry Hill shouted.

Giggling, we rolled up our untouched second

fiber bars in a napkin. Cherry Hill tossed them silently across the room toward the trash can. Two points!

On Friday nights, my sister, Tina, would sleep on the couch downstairs so that Cherry Hill could sleep over in our room. Cherry Hill loved Friday nights at my house because they were such a blast. That's the night my dad brought home junk food and video movies and we all got to stay up till midnight or even later to watch them all.

On this particular Friday night, my dad strode into the house carrying a bucket of Kentucky Fried Chicken, three movies, and a small jar containing an enormous cockroach.

My mom, Cherry Hill, and I squealed "E-yew!" in disgust.

"You didn't find that at Kentucky Fried, did you, Phil?" my mom asked with a shudder.

My dad laughed. "No. Bobby found it and saved it for me." Bobby was the janitor at the downtown office building where my dad worked.

Cameron came into the kitchen and started digging in the chicken bucket for a drumstick.

My mom swatted his hand away. "Wait'll we get set up in the family room," she said, grabbing some paper plates from the cupboard. Cherry Hill and I got napkins and silverware.

Cameron spotted the cockroach. Our cat, Brandy, had jumped up on the counter and was nosing the jar. "Dad, you didn't bring that thing home for . . ." His voice trailed off ominously.

My mom turned around wearing a bright smile. "Oh, did I forget to mention that the Chases are coming over for dinner tomorrow night?"

Cameron and I groaned. "Yes, Mother, you did conveniently forget to mention that little fact," I said.

My mom's fellow professor and office mate, Larry Chase, and his wife and kids came for dinner—or we went to their house—several times a year. The adults always had a grand old time. It was us kids who suffered. The Chases had a son Cam's age, but Otis was absolutely obsessed with bugs and not at all interested in the stuff Cameron and his friends were interested in. Their daughter, Casey, was in my class at school. She had a long, drawn-out, boring opinion about *everything*.

"Otis bugs me," Cameron said, following us into the family room.

My mom burst out laughing. "Oh, *bad* pun." The rest of us roared. Even Cameron smiled in spite of himself.

Soon all six of us—even Tina, who actually acted like a member of the family on Friday nights—were in front of the blaring television, swigging Pepsis, gnawing on chicken, and watching an old Disney movie about an absentminded professor who invents this stuff that makes it possible for him to jump a hundred feet in the air. Between movies, we talked about *The Room 11 Video News*, and about a guy who had fainted right in the middle of my mom's English composition class, and about the fake bomb threat someone phoned in to my dad's office building. Before we knew it, it was 10 o'clock and time for the Channel 9 *Eyewitness News.*

"There was another major earthquake in Iran today, Stan," Dianna Duvall said with a bright smile.

Tina groaned. "Do me a favor, Cherry Hill. Two favors, actually. When you do your school's news, don't smile when you talk about something bad. And don't don't *don't* pretend like you're giving the news to your co-anchor instead of to the audience. I mean, don't say, 'And that's our news for today, Maureen.' "

"It's *Marina*," Cherry Hill said. "Marina Dobbs is the other anchor kid."

"Oh, yeah," Tina said. "Marina." She handed me the box of bran cereal that was making the rounds and I shook out a handful. My crazy mother: We could eat the worst junk food and she wouldn't bat an eye as long as we ate some fiber afterward. It was like the fiber would cancel out everything else.

"Don't worry about Cherry Hill acting buddy-buddy with Marina Dobbs on the air," I said. "She can't stand Marina."

Everyone turned to Cherry Hill. "I think Stan Malomar is as much an airhead as Dianna Duvall," she said, nodding at the anchorman on the TV screen. "It's pretty sexist that everyone rips on her but not on him."

Her changing the subject and not agreeing about Marina gave me the same strange twinge of annoyance and jealousy I'd felt after the election when she'd been acting like Marina.

After breakfast Saturday morning, Cherry Hill shocked me by suggesting that we play Barbies. Mine hadn't seen the light of day in all those weeks since Cherry Hill had come back from Colorado and announced she would never play Barbies again. *Très bébé*, you know.

I didn't say anything, just followed her back upstairs to my room. She pulled the Dream House down from the shelf in my closet. The truth was, I really hadn't missed playing Barbies at all. The last few times we had played with them, way back in fifth grade, it had been pretty boring.

"You can't just spend all day trying on clothes and getting ready for dates, Barbie," my doll had said to hers in exasperation. "Get a life. Better yet, get a *job*. We do have bills to pay, you know. Such as the rent on this fabulous Dream House."

Her Barbie got all huffy. "I don't need a job, Barbette," she snapped. (Cherry Hill had insisted that both of the dolls couldn't be named Barbie and I had lost the coin toss.) "We've got very wealthy parents."

I was always trying to get her Barbie to go horseback riding with mine on plastic horses from my sister's old collection. We used to do that a lot, but one day Cherry Hill refused. "They look ridiculous on those horses," she'd said.

Well, yeah, the horses were a little on the small side and Barbie and Barbette's feet dragged on the ground when they rode them. But at least they were doing something besides looking at their clothes in the Dream House closet.

Now I opened up the Dream House and pulled our dolls from the living room where they'd been prisoners for four months. (Cherry Hill always kept her Barbie at my house because I had a Dream House while she only had a Shoe Box.) Setting up the patio and pool area, I propped my Barbette on a chaise longue and prepared to be bored stiff.

But Cherry Hill pleasantly surprised me. "Let's get jobs today, Barbette," she said, rolling Barbette off the chaise longue and into the cardboard pool.

"Doing what?" I asked.

"The news, of course."

We fashioned an anchor desk out of an overturned Kleenex box and sat the Barbies behind it on two stools from the Barbie Soda Shoppe.

"Good evening," Cherry Hill's Barbie said to an imaginary camera. "There was a shoot-out at the mall today, but no one was injured. Also, seven tigers escaped from the San Diego Zoo and are still at large. And the mayor has declared that Monday will be Child Appreciation Day in San Diego. There will be no school and forcing your child to do any chore will be illegal. Law-breaking parents will be confined to the penitentiary for not less than one year."

"Hey, wait a minute," my Barbette said. "I didn't get to say anything!"

Cherry Hill burst out laughing. "Of course not," she said. "You're playing Marina the Mannequin."

Cheerfully, I pulled Barbette's head to the left. "Oh?" I made her say.

CHAPTER THREE

Later that afternoon, my dad dropped us off at the mall. Cherry Hill and I did what we usually did: We went into a few stores together and then we separated for a few minutes. I went in the bookstore and she went across the way to an accessories store. The store was called Baubles, but they might just as well have called themselves Earrings, because that's all they had. About eight million of them, and 7,999,999 of those were *pierced* earrings. It was a very boring store if you didn't have pierced ears, and I didn't. My mom refused to let Tina or me have our ears pierced till we were sixteen, and I was secretly glad. The idea of having holes drilled made my earlobes tremble.

I bought a paperback filled with short stories

written by Anne Frank while she was a teen hiding from the Nazis. Then I sat on the bench in front of the bookstore, which was our agreed-upon meeting place. It had been on this very bench, a few months earlier, that I had seen Marina Dobbs with her two blond and beautiful older sisters. Marina had had a pouty, rejected look on her face and was whining about something as she tagged along after them.

They were just completely ignoring her. She looked exactly how I probably looked when Tina and her friends were forced to take me with them somewhere. I'm glad she didn't see me because my mouth was hanging open in surprise. The regal Marina Dobbs was somebody's mistreated, ignored, barely tolerated little sister! Just like the rest of us! I'd even found myself feeling a little sorry for her, although my sympathy waned when I got to school the following Monday and she acted as snooty as ever. Still, any mystique she held for me had shattered that day at the mall and never again did I act worshipful in her presence, like everyone else but Cherry Hill did.

"Hey! Wake up and move on!" boomed a deep voice beside me. I jumped. Cherry Hill plopped down next to me, laughing.

"I wasn't sleeping, I was thinking," I said.

"Same thing," Cherry Hill said with a grin, snapping her gum.

Our next stop was my favorite place in the mall—the food court. As usual, we ordered curly fries and Cokes and sat at a table that gave us a good view of everybody else. Then we played our Name Game.

Cherry Hill dipped a curly fry in ketchup and nudged me. With her chin, she gestured toward a couple a few tables away. Both had lots of freckles. "Pongo and Perdita," she said.

I burst out laughing, and Coke sprayed out through my nose. Pongo and Perdita were the mother and father dogs in *101 Dalmatians*.

Suddenly, the elderly couple at the table next to us erupted into an argument. "You are so cheap, Harold!" the woman said. "You have pinched every penny you ever made, and I'm sick of it! I'm sick of having cheap dishes, crummy cookware, linens that don't last a year, and these greasy fast-food lunches! And furthermore—"

"Calm down, Winnie," the man interrupted.

"Winnie the Shrew," I whispered to Cherry Hill. It was her turn to crack up.

She showed me the earrings she'd bought—dangling hearts made of fake turquoise. "Pretty," I said.

I brought out the Anne Frank book. "Want to read it when I'm done?" I asked.

She shook her head. "It makes me too depressed that she dies."

"But this isn't the story about *her*—these are stories she wrote," I said.

"I know. But knowing that she died not long after she wrote the stories would make me too sad."

I nodded my understanding. We sat for a few minutes in a melancholy but companionable silence. Suddenly, Mrs. Summers bustled up, laden with shopping bags.

"I knew I'd find you here," she said, sitting down. She usually picked us up out in front of Sears, but she explained that she'd had some shopping of her own to do.

"Want to come over for dinner?" she asked me.

"No, thanks. The Chases are coming for dinner." I rolled my eyes.

Cherry Hill and her mother laughed. They were used to my complaints about the Chases.

"Better bone up on politics," Mrs. Summers said.

"Better bone up on *everything*," Cherry Hill corrected. "You never know *what* Casey Chase is going to come up with."

25

At six that evening, the Chases showed up with a bouquet of flowers, a bottle of wine, and Otis's ant farm.

"Play with that out on the patio, okay, dear?" my mom said. Cameron followed Otis outside grudgingly, playing "a good little host" as my mother had ordered him to in the minutes before the doorbell rang.

Casey was wearing a T-shirt with a big peace symbol splashed on the front and I prepared myself for a couple of hours of her ranting and raving about a civil war in some obscure African country. Casey Chase was one of those people who always had a cause. She often showed up at school wearing a black armband or carrying a sheaf of brochures about some endangered fish. She brought her lunch to school in a canvas bag that read I SAVED A TREE TODAY! as if it took a whole tree to make one little lunch sack. Our fifth-grade teacher, Mr. Small, used to call her Make-a-Case Chase, because she could take a stand about *anything* and turn it into a major issue. I once heard her make an impassioned speech about what a ripoff it was that hot dogs come ten to a package but buns only come in eights, resulting in two bunless wieners unless you bought *two* bags of buns, in which case you'd then have six wienerless buns left over.

It's not that I wasn't interested in saving trees or that the hot dog-bun ripoff didn't sort of annoy me too. But when somebody is that strident and intense every single second you're with her . . . well, being with her was very tiring.

But that Saturday evening, to my surprise, she was pleasant and quiet during dinner—except to shout "Boycott!" when my mom asked if anyone wanted salt or pepper. (Everyone was smart enough not to ask her what was behind that outburst.)

After dinner, she just smiled and followed me and Tina upstairs when I suggested a game of Monopoly.

"You play with them, Tina," my mom called after us.

"I sure will," Tina said sweetly. But the minute we got into the room we shared she took the phone into the walk-in closet and shut the door behind her, warning us, "Keep the noise down."

It was after we got the Monopoly board set up and I had rolled the dice that Casey hit me with her latest cause.

"I wanted to say how sorry I am that Mrs. Desideri didn't choose you to be weather person," she said.

My mouth dropped open.

She reached over and patted my shoulder. "I know how badly you wanted the job."

I narrowed my eyes at her. "Wait just a minute. How did *you* know that?"

She tossed her head of springy red ringlets. "I saw all the suggestion sheets everyone turned in," she said.

I stood up angrily. "Mrs. Desideri let you read them? She had no right to—"

Casey waved her hands. "I only saw them because I empty several classroom wastebaskets after school and take all the papers to the recycling center."

"Oh." I sat down, trying to hide how embarrassed I felt that she knew one of my innermost desires. "It's no big deal."

Casey gave us each two hundred dollars for passing Go. "I'd say it is. In fact, I'd say there's much more to it than you know."

"What do you mean?" I landed on one of the railroads and bought it.

"You know why you didn't get the job?" she asked.

I shook my head.

"It's because you have braces."

I gasped. Automatically, my hand flew up to cover my metallic mouth.

"Desideri didn't want anyone with braces in front of the camera," Casey said. "It'd make *The Room 11 Video News* look like some amateurish elementary school production."

"But that's what it *is,* Casey," I said.

"I know. But she doesn't want it to *look* that way. Who knows? She just might be planning to use a tape of our show to get her own foot in the door at a *real* TV station. To get a job as a television producer or something."

I laughed. "Don't be ridiculous." I couldn't imagine Mrs. Desideri doing anything but teaching.

"I'm not being ridiculous," Casey said, rolling the dice.

"How'd you ever come up with that weird theory anyway?" I asked.

"Well, let me tell you something, Rachel. Almost all of the boys wanted to be the sports reporter. And almost all of the girls wanted to be the anchor kids. You were the only—and I mean only—person who asked to be the weather person. And yet she didn't give it to you. She gave it to David Jenks, who is gorgeous but has an IQ of about three. Why did Mrs. Desideri do that? Because she's a looksist."

"A what?"

"A looksist. You know how a sexist is someone who favors males over females?"

I nodded.

"A looksist is someone who favors good-looking people over everyone else," Casey said. She bought Baltic Avenue.

I rolled the dice and landed in jail. "Then almost everyone in our class is a looksist," I said. "After all, they elected the two prettiest girls as the anchor kids."

Casey nodded. "You're absolutely right. If they'd voted for the two smartest kids, which they should have, you and I would be the anchor kids, kid."

I bit my lip to hide a flattered smile, then rolled the dice and got out of jail.

"The thing is, I don't blame the kids in our class," Casey said. "After all, they're too young to know any better."

I laughed. She seemed to have forgotten the fact that she was eleven-going-on-twelve just like the rest of us.

"But Mrs. Desideri's looksism is unforgivable," Casey continued, buying Park Place. "This video news project is supposed to be a learning experience. Not some slick showcase."

I bought Boardwalk. "I think you've blown this

way out of proportion. And I don't even think you're right."

"I knew you wouldn't believe me. Here's proof." Casey got up on her knees and pulled a folded piece of paper from her jeans pocket. Solemnly, she presented it to me.

It was my suggestion sheet. Next to where I'd printed "Weather girl" as my first, second, and third job choices, Mrs. Desideri had scribbled a note to herself: "No. Has bcs."

"B C S," I said aloud.

"An abbreviation for braces," Casey said.

Anger at Mrs. Desideri flooded my body.

Casey patted my shoulder again. "You know I'm going to be doing opinion commentaries on the *Video News*, right?"

"Yeah," I muttered. I counted my paper money, slapping it down hard on top of the Monopoly box.

"Well, I'm just giving you fair warning that I intend to devote my first commentary to this incident. I intend to expose Mrs. Desideri for what she is. A looksist."

I threw down the little hat I'd been using as a marker. "No! She'll think I put you up to it."

"Oh, come on. She knows we're not friends." We both blushed and looked down at the game board. Here our parents had been friends for years and we still were little more than acquaintances. As far as I knew Casey didn't have any friends and didn't seem to have time for friends anyway. She was too busy being tiresome.

Tina, in the closet, suddenly screamed with laughter at something the person on the other end of the line had said. It broke our awkward silence.

"You have nothing to lose and everything to gain," Casey said. "Once I expose her motive on our first broadcast, she'll almost be obligated to give you the weather person spot on future newscasts."

I thought about it and then nodded slowly. No one would think I put Casey up to this. Everybody knew Casey Chase needed no encouragement to get all riled up about something.

"There's just one little thing . . ." Casey said with utmost casualness.

A little warning bell went off in my head and I stifled a groan. "Okay, what's the catch, Casey?" I asked.

"I want you to write my script."

"Me?"

"Yeah. You're probably the best writer in the class. That essay you wrote about how sad the day after Christmas is . . . that was great."

I laughed, embarrassed. "That was so corny. I thought the kids would puke when Mrs. Desideri read it aloud."

"Corn can be very nutritious," Casey said.

I did the finger-down-throat gesture at the corniness of that remark.

She grinned and put a house on Baltic. "Well, what do you say? Will you help me write it?"

I bought another railroad. "Casey, I don't get it. You're never at a loss for words."

"Except when I'm faced with a blank piece of paper," she said. "I'm a real whiz verbally, but I panic when it comes to putting it in writing. And I have to submit my commentary in writing to Mrs. Desideri. Come on, Rach. Help me out."

"But what if she reads it and refuses to let you do it on the air?"

"She wouldn't dare. That would make this an even bigger scandal. Come on. Say yes."

"Mrs. Desideri will never find out I helped you?" I asked.

"Never. I will take the secret to my grave."

"Come on down for dessert, you guys!" my mom called from out in the hall. She was rattling the cereal box.

"Oh, all right," I said in answer to both of them.

CHAPTER FOUR

Every day the following week, during the hour before lunch, we split up into assignment groups to start working on the first edition of *The Room 11 Video News.*

"Okay, you guys, what have you come up with for potential news stories?" I asked Betsy Smith and Julie Kooda, the other news writers, on Tuesday. We were huddled in a corner of the classroom. The other groups had claimed areas of their own.

Betsy opened her notebook. "Maintenance staff paints new white lines in the parking lot," she read. "Room One's Mrs. King gives birth to her third baby boy. Cafeteria switches hot dogs to Fridays and macaroni and cheese to Thursdays."

I groaned. "That's it?"

Betsy nodded and closed her notebook.

I looked at Julie. "What have you got?"

Julie took a piece of notebook paper from her pocket and unfolded it slowly. "Stray dog chases kids on playground but leaves when custodian sprays hose at it," she read. "Rock thrown through window of Room Six over the weekend. Room Eight goes on field trip to the tidepools." She looked up at me with a shy smile as she carefully refolded the paper.

I buried my face in my hands and groaned again. "If we do the stories you guys suggest, we'll have to change the name to *The Room 11 Video Snooze*."

Betsy and Julie giggled. They thought I was hilarious. I guess that's why they had elected me head news writer at our first meeting the day before. That and the fact that I was the one who had finally said "What should we do?" We'd just been sitting there staring at our fingernails.

I glared at them now. "It isn't funny! We only have three more days to get all our stories written. On Monday, we have to give copies to Cherry Hill and Marina and the camera crew. And the stuff you just read me is the most boring stuff I ever heard. Borrring!"

Julie raised her hand as if I were the teacher. "But, but—"

"How do you think we're going to fill a whole hour?" I rolled right over her. "Should we have the camera crew shoot ten minutes worth of video of the white lines in the parking lot? Another five minutes of a rock laying on the floor in Room Six?"

My sarcasm was getting to them. Betsy looked crushed. Julie looked a little angry. "Well, what did *you* come up with, Rachel?" she squeaked. "You were supposed to come up with some human interest features."

I ducked my head and laughed nervously. "Well, this isn't exactly *human* interest," I said, "but I think we should do a story about Veronica Sheldon's parrot, Mr. Sam. She's taught him how to roller skate."

Julie waved a hand. "I've seen him at birthday parties. He's not very good."

I'd seen Mr. Sam at a birthday party once too. He mostly just stood around looking bored in the special little parrot skates Veronica had designed for him. But at least doing a story about him would give me the chance to write some funny lines like "Veronica Sheldon had an idea everyone said would never fly." And "When Veronica bought Mr. Sam, she didn't know she was getting a *wheel deal*." Cherry Hill would get a big kick out of reading a story like that on the air. She could even lead into the next story with "Rolling right along. . . ."

"That's *all* you've got?" Julie asked.

I put my nose in the air. "No, that's not all," I said haughtily. "It just so happens there's a fifth-grader—Ryan Fleming, he's in Room Six with my brother—who was staying in a hotel right next to the Berlin Wall when the German people started pulling it down a few years ago and put an end to communism."

Betsy and Julie gasped. "Really?"

"Did he help knock it down?" Betsy asked. "Did he get a piece?"

"Did he dance on top of the wall all night?" Julie asked. "I remember seeing some people on the news doing that."

"I can't divulge that until he agrees to tell his story on camera," I said. "He's not sure he wants to go public with it. Apparently, it's quite a sentimental story. Very close to his heart." The truth was—I hadn't even spoken to the guy yet and knew only that he'd been in Berlin when it happened.

Betsy and Julie nodded solemnly.

"Look, Julie," I said, "you work on the tidepool field trip story. At least the camera crew can get some pretty footage of La Jolla Cove. And Betsy, instead of just doing the hot dogs/macaroni and cheese switch, why don't you work on a story about how the cafeteria decides what to serve? I mean besides just striving to invent dishes that will most resemble barf."

They giggled again, but I felt depressed. Despite the changes and suggestions I'd made, *The Room 11 Video News* still sounded like one big yawn so far.

Mrs. Desideri strolled up to our group. "I just wanted to make something clear to you three," she said in a confidential whisper. "Without your writing, there'd be nothing for the anchor kids to say, and, hence, no broadcast. That's why, though your job may not be the most glamorous, it's the most important."

I know she expected me to smile in appreciation, but I couldn't muster one, remembering her "Has bcs" comment.

She moved on to the next group, the editors, who would put the various stories into some order after they were filmed. "I bet she says that to every group," I said to Julie and Betsy under my breath. They cracked up, but it didn't make me feel any better.

"Let's use the rest of the time to come up with questions to ask the various people we'll be interviewing," I said.

Betsy and Julie went to work. Idly, I glanced over at Cherry Hill. She and Marina were sitting together near the front of the classroom. Surprised, I looked at them again. Their heads were bent close together and they were whispering like old friends. When they'd had their first meeting yesterday, they had pretty much spent the hour yawning at each other and doodling in their separate notebooks.

Marina said something that made Cherry Hill throw back her head and laugh. What did they have to talk about, let alone laugh about? They didn't have any news to talk about, since we hadn't yet written it. They didn't have any video to talk about since the camera crew couldn't film any stories till we wrote them. They didn't have a set to talk about, since the set design crew hadn't even started building it. In fact, why was Mrs. Desideri making Cherry Hill and Marina have a meeting at all? Now I *really* felt in the pits.

A couple of minutes before lunch, I waited out in front of Room Six. When the bell rang, fifth-graders streamed out the door.

I stopped a skinny red-headed kid. "You Ryan Fleming?" I asked.

"Who wants to know?"

"Rachel Harper, *Room 11 Video News.*" *Oh, wow. Did that sound impressive or what?*

To Ryan, I guess not. "So what?" He started to leave.

I blocked his way and whipped out a notebook and pen. "We're considering doing a story about you and your experiences at the Berlin Wall. I need you to answer a few questions. First, what were you doing over there in the first place?"

"My dad was doing some kind of business."

"What kind?"

"I dunno. Ask him."

"Never mind. Um . . . how close did you come to the Berlin Wall?"

"We could see it out our hotel window," he said.

"Really?" I tried to keep cool. This might really be an exciting story. "So what happened on the day the Berlin Wall came down?"

"I don't remember."

"You don't remember? You don't remember one of the most important events of this whole century?"

His face turned as red as his hair. "Give me a break. I was just a little kid."

I took a step closer to him. Maybe he thought I was going to hit him or something, because he waved his hands in my face. "Okay, okay, wait," he said. "I do remember a coupla things. I remember that it was real noisy down in the street. People shouting and singing and honking and stuff. It was so noisy I couldn't sleep."

My heart sank. He hadn't gone down to the street. "What else do you remember?"

"I remember me and my dad trying to order breakfast in the hotel restaurant the next morning. Only there weren't any waitresses. They were all over at the wall celebrating. It was real crummy."

"But didn't you feel *thrilled* by all that? All that history taking place before your very eyes? Didn't you feel awed? Dizzy? Incredible? How did you feel?"

"I felt tired because I didn't get much sleep, and hungry 'cause I didn't get any breakfast, okay?" He started backing off down the hall.

"Don't call us—we'll call you!" I snapped, crossing his name off the story idea list.

Just then, a bunch of kids from Room 11 came around the corner, heading for the cafeteria. *Oh, great.* Glenn Vandever was among them. As he approached me, his face lit up with the nicest smile. I felt the corners of my lips begin to quiver, so I clamped them closed and stretched them across my face.

Glenn stopped smiling and passed me, looking a little puzzled and hurt.

Cherry Hill and Marina were right behind him. Cherry Hill stopped beside me. Marina walked on. "You've got a toothache?" Cherry Hill asked me.

"No. Why?"

"You were grimacing."

"I was not. I was smiling at Glenn Vandever."

She snickered. "I'd hate to see you *frown* at him. Nightmare on Elm Street!"

"Very funny," I said. "Aren't you going to eat lunch with your new best friend, *Marina Dobbs*?"

Cherry Hill grabbed my arm and started steering me toward the cafeteria. "Speaking of Marina the Mannequin, she has absolutely the worst breath," Cherry Hill said, holding her nose daintily. "It smells like a wet dog."

"Really? Did you tell her that? Oh, knowing you, I'm sure you did."

"I simply said, out of nowhere, 'I gargle with Listerine every morning.' I'm sure she took the hint."

"What'd she say?"

Cherry Hill leaned her face close to mine. " 'Oh?' " she said, blasting my face with her breath. "I nearly keeled over."

And I doubled over and cracked up.

Casey Chase called me that night. "Can you talk?" she whispered. She seemed to be taking to heart her vow to keep our deal secret.

"Yeah, it's okay," I said. Tina was down the hall taking a bath. I opened my notebook. "Look," I said to Casey, "all I've got so far is your definition of what a looksist is. What else did you want to include?"

"Well, say something about how Mrs. Desideri shouldn't be pulling this kind of thing at a school."

"Casey, you put that beautifully the other night. Can't you remember how you said it?"

"No!" she groaned. "I told you—I panic when confronted with a blank piece of paper."

"But *you're* not confronting a blank piece of paper. *I* am."

She wailed something and I tuned her out and thought hard. Finally, I remembered. "I know how you put it: 'The video news hour is supposed to be a learning experience, not a slick showcase.' "

"Yes!" Casey shrieked. "Now just elaborate on that a little, okay? Bye!"

"Wait a minute, Casey! Your commentary is supposed to last three minutes. I can't come up with that much without more help from you."

She was silent.

"Look, why don't you just rant and rave into a tape recorder for a few minutes?" I suggested. "Then give me the tape tomorrow."

Casey blew out a sigh of relief. "That is a fantastic idea. Oh, Rachel, you won't regret this. Weather person, here you come!"

CHAPTER FIVE

"**R**achel Harper has an announcement to make," Mrs. Desideri said after Social Studies the next morning.

Few things terrify me more than making a speech in front of the class. But we were desperate.

I went to the front of the room. "Betsy, Julie, and I need your help coming up with story leads for *The Room 11 Video News*," I squeaked.

Then I noticed that Glenn Vandever was smiling at me. Instantly, I changed my quivering lips into rattlesnake lips. I fixed my gaze on a fluorescent light on the ceiling. "What we need most are ideas for *news* stories," I managed to force out from between my tightly pressed lips. "Incidents that have happened here at school."

"Hey, excuse me! But we're down here!" Benny McVie called out. Several kids snickered.

I ignored him and kept my eyes focused on the ceiling. "Like how someone threw a rock through the window of Room Six. Only more dramatic than that. Something we can get on video."

Josh Taylor apparently raised his hand.

"Yes, Josh?" said Mrs. Desideri.

"We could reenact the crime like they do on *America's Most Wanted*," he said. "I'd be happy to be the one to throw the rock."

Practically every other boy in the class shouted, "No, I'll do it!"

"No way," said Mrs. Desideri, laughing. "No reenactments! Continue, Rachel."

"We can use human interest story ideas too," I said to the ceiling. "Stuff like how Ryan Fleming, who's a fifth-grader, was at the Berlin Wall when it came down." I used it as an example even though I knew we weren't going to do the story. "But we need news most of all. I'll pass around this box, and if you have an idea, just jot it down and throw it in."

I held up the box and suddenly felt embarrassed about it. I'd let my mom decorate the box and she'd gotten horribly cute. She'd made each letter in the words STORY IDEAS into a little picture of something that started with that letter. The *T,* for example, was a telephone pole. *O* was an orange. *R* was a railroad track. And the *S,* appropriately enough, was a snake.

Fortunately, no one laughed. A few kids wrote stuff down on pieces of paper and stuffed them into the box as it made its rounds. I slunk back to my seat. Mrs. Desideri had us break into our video news groups.

Betsy brought the box over to our little corner of the room and the three of us ripped into it eagerly.

The first piece of paper I opened read: "How come you were trying to talk with your mouth closed? Are you practicing to be a ventriloquist or what?" I recognized Cherry Hill's big roundish handwriting.

I looked over to where she was sitting with Marina. She was grinning at me.

"Very funny," I mouthed.

Cherry Hill turned away and smiled at Marina. They bent their heads together and started chatting away as if they were the best of friends.

I had a sudden brilliant idea and raised my hand. Mrs. Desideri came over. "Can Cherry Hill join our group today?" I asked. "We'd like to run some of these suggestions past an anchor kid for her reaction." That would certainly break up their little chat fest.

Mrs. Desideri looked over at Marina and Cherry Hill. "Let me ask her." She walked over to them, and I watched them talk. The teacher came back to me. "They say they're discussing whether they should sit or stand while they give the news, and how long to pause between each story. They say they can't spare any time to help you today."

"I didn't ask for *them*, I asked for Cherry Hill," I muttered to Mrs. Desideri's back as she went to help another group.

Casey Chase got up and headed for the pencil sharpener. When she was behind my chair, she pretended to drop her pencil, uttering a loud, phony-sounding, and totally unnecessary "Oh, clumsy me!" I felt my jacket, slung over the back of the chair, move slightly. Casey was no doubt shoving her tape into the pocket. This hush-hush top-secret spy stuff of hers was *so* corny.

I went back to reading the story leads in the box. There were eleven of them, but only three had possibilities. And they were all human interest stories instead of news:

1. Brittany Fitzhugh, a former Kennedy Elementary student who was now in ninth grade at Lewis Junior High, had invented a toothbrush holder that also cleans the brush. The invention had won second prize at the statewide Student Inventors Fair.

2. The mother of Greg Malcolm, a first-grader, had won $500,000 in the California State Lottery. The Malcolms were building a huge new house on McIver Drive with the money.

3. Devon Gonzalez's seventeen-year-old sister Lena had been a runner-up in the recent Miss San Diego pageant.

I felt depressed again. It wasn't that these stories were boring. They were actually sort of interesting. It was just that they weren't about Kennedy Elementary students. They were about used-to-be Kennedy Elementary students. Or relatives of Kennedy Elementary students.

I found myself standing up and croaking to the classroom at large, "You people listen up! We need more ideas! Please! Please put your thinking caps on and help us!"

I plopped back into my chair, mortified. What had possessed me to get up like that? And why, why, *why* had I made that corny, corny, shades-of-*Sesame-Street* thinking cap remark? *Très bébé.* My face was burning.

Twenty minutes later, my face was *still* burning. I finally figured it out: I was in the crazed clutches of some sort of fever. I was sick! *That's* what had possessed me. My throat felt as if I had scraped the length of it with a fork.

I raised my hand and Mrs. Desideri came over. "I think I'm sick," I whispered.

She packed me off to the nurse's office. Cherry Hill was still so busy giggling and talking with Marina that she didn't even notice when I left.

The halls were deserted. In my fevered state, I had the wild urge to write "Mrs. Desideri is secretly a man!" or something equally outrageous on the wall . . . just for the news value. I even pictured Cherry Hill interviewing one of the teacher's five children: "It's the public's right to know—does your mother shave every morning?" I laughed hysterically.

Luckily, just as I started to take a Magic Marker out of my book bag, the door to Room 9 opened and a kid with a bathroom pass came out. I shoved the pen back into my bag and continued on.

The nurse took my temperature. It was 103. She had me sit in a chair by the window while I waited for my dad to drive in from downtown to pick me up.

The lunch bell rang as I was sitting there. I watched Cherry Hill walk to the cafeteria with Marina. They were probably going to eat lunch together. I felt too sick to care.

My dad was worried that I might have strep

throat, so he took me to the doctor. But it turned out I just had some nasty bug that my dear little brother, Cameron, had brought home from Room 6. Cam was the disgustingly healthy type who just sneezed three or four times—spreading the virus around—and then he was over it. Then the rest of us would get it and practically die.

Since it wasn't strep, the doctor didn't prescribe any medicine. "Just take the next couple of days off school, drink plenty of fluids, and sleep as much as you can," she said.

On the way home, my dad stopped at the pharmacy and bought me some cough drops. Not those sweet, tasty little cherry-flavored jobs but big macho ones—as my mom would later call them—that tasted gaggably like hardened Vick's VapoRub. I complained and whined and made hideous faces when my dad insisted I try one. Just between us, though, those cough drops made my throat feel a lot better.

For the next three days I lay around popping cough drops, blowing my nose, reading my latest batch of library books, watching an occasional *I Love Lucy,* and worrying about the video news project.

Cherry Hill called after school on both Thursday and Friday. When I casually asked her who she was eating lunch with, she just as casually answered

"Leslie and Kim." She never even mentioned Marina. On Friday, she reported that my fellow news writers, Julie and Betsy, had been utterly lost without me.

"When we split into groups today, they just sat there and stared at each other," Cherry Hill said.

I got off the phone with her and called up both Julie and Betsy. I ordered them to write their stories—Julie's on the tidepool field trip and Betsy's on the cafeteria menu—over the weekend. "I want the finished stories in my hands at nine A.M. Monday," I barked.

Julie was pretty annoyed. She had been planning to go camping over the weekend.

"Look, we have to turn *something* in to the camera crew and the anchor kids on Monday," I said. "You're lucky I'm not assigning you more than one story."

"What about *your* story?" Julie asked. "What are *you* going to be doing?"

"I'm . . . I've scheduled an interview with the . . . um . . . Malcolm family about their lottery winnings and their new house on Sunday," I lied. "My story will be ready to turn in on Monday. I'm even typing it."

On Sunday, I dragged my weak body out of bed and wrote Casey's commentary, based on the tape she'd stuck in my jacket pocket. Then I went down to McIver Drive where the Malcolms were building and prayed that they'd be there even though the house wasn't finished and they hadn't moved in yet. By sheer luck, Greg's dad and his big brother Todd were out in front planting a tree.

I whipped open my notebook and interviewed them. Mr. Malcolm was really irritating. He kept calling me Little Miss Vanna White. I guess he was confusing the *Wheel of Fortune* lady with Dianna Duvall of *Eyewitness News.* But I didn't correct him. I figured if I did he might get mad or embarrassed and stop talking to me.

Finally, I asked my last question: "How did Mrs. Malcolm choose the lottery numbers that won?"

"She just used the ages of everyone in our family," Mr. Malcolm said. "Two, six, nine, thirteen, thirty-eight, and forty-four. Got that, Little Miss Vanna White?"

I said thanks, slammed my notebook shut, and started running up the street. I looked back. "Hey, Vanna White is a letter turner! She's not a reporter!" I shouted at them.

Mr. Malcolm shouted something in return. I couldn't hear what it was exactly, but he sounded mad.

I didn't care. I had my story. Just call me Rachel Reporter.

CHAPTER SIX

Marina Dobbs called me something else on Monday morning.

"Incompetent!" she said to me with her eyes flashing. I guess it would have stung more except that I was busy being stunned that she was actually showing some emotion at school. Obviously, *The Room 11 Video News* was much more important to her than she'd led us all to believe.

"How are we supposed to fill a whole show with three little stories?" Marina continued, shaking the papers I'd handed to her in my face. "And they aren't even interesting stories. 'Our Trip to the Tidepools.'" She read the title of Julie's story in an excruciatingly boring monotone. "Give me a break!"

"Now, Marina," said Mrs. Desideri, "we still have a week before the *Video News* will be shown in the classrooms. Surely the girls will come up with more stories before that. And what they've come up with so far is a good start." But she looked disappointed too.

"Not in my opinion," Marina snapped.

"*The Room 11 Video Snooze*," Cherry Hill said, and the camera crew—Janie, Porter, and Annie—cracked up.

I glared at her. I'd told her about breaking up the news writers with that Video Snooze crack and she was stealing it without giving me any credit.

I felt a twinge of dismay that Julie's and Betsy's stories were on the blah side, but I was still excited about my own. My first few lines were in the form of a poem:

Two, six, nine, thirteen,
Thirty-eight, and forty-four:
These are the numbers the Malcolms used
And they went on to score!

They won five hundred thousand bucks
And that sure ain't no jive
They're using the money to build a house
Over on McIver Drive!

Marina glanced over my piece and then thrust it back at me. "Get real. Newscasters aren't rap artists. They don't rhyme their stories! *Très bébé.*"

I couldn't believe it. The great Marina was picking up that dumb, *incorrect* expression of Cherry Hill's.

Mrs. Desideri came to my defense. "Rachel is not going to tell you how to do your job, Marina. So I don't want you telling her how to do hers. You and Cherry Hill will read the news as the girls write it."

Cherry Hill sent me a secret little victorious smile. I returned it.

"Oh?" Marina said, head cocked. "Then you get the lottery story, Cherry Hill."

"Fine," Cherry Hill said. "I think it's cute."

"Okay," Mrs. Desideri said, getting up as the lunch bell rang. "We'll film the tidepool story tomorrow after school, the lottery story Wednesday after school, and the cafeteria story on Thursday morning. Meanwhile, you news writers should keep your eyes open for more stories. In fact, we all will."

Casey Chase came up beside the teacher. "My commentary, Mrs. Desideri," she said, handing over a file folder. That's how I'd slipped the commentary to Casey before school that morning, having gotten up at six to type it on my mom's computer so it couldn't be traced to me. It had taken forever.

The teacher beamed at Casey. "Very good! I'll read it tonight and get back to you about it tomorrow."

My throat still felt pretty raw, so I popped a cough drop on the way to lunch that day.

"Hi, Rachel," Glenn Vandever said, smiling as he walked past Cherry Hill and me.

I smiled back.

What? I smiled back? How had I managed that? And then I became aware that I was still sucking on the cough drop. It seemed that as long as my mouth was busy doing something else, I could aim a beautific smile at Glenn with absolutely no problem!

Later that afternoon, when the final bell rang, I decided to test my theory. I popped a cough drop in my mouth and stayed in my seat until Glenn stood up and walked past me. He smiled. And I smiled back! He looked pleased.

I sat impatiently through my regular monthly orthodontist appointment that afternoon, then raced home. "Mom, I need more cough drops," I said. "My throat is still kind of scratchy."

She put a hand on my forehead and peered at me with narrowed eyes. "I think we'd better go back to the doctor, young lady," she said. "You just can't seem to shake this bug."

"Oh, no, really, Mom, I'm getting better and better every day. Can't you just give me maybe four more days' worth of cough drops?" I was thinking that that would tide me over till I got my allowance on Saturday and was able to go to the store and buy my own supply of cough drops or hard candy or *something*. "I'm sure I'll be completely over this by the weekend."

My mom went to her bathroom and came back with a handful of the little sweeties. I slipped them into the pocket of my jean jacket.

Before school the next morning, Mrs. Desideri came out to the playground where I was standing with Cherry Hill and a few other girls and asked me to please come to Room 11 for "a little talk." She did not look pleased. She marched along in front of me without a word.

When I saw Casey sitting in the classroom waiting for us, I knew immediately what this was all about. Casey wouldn't look at me.

Mrs. Desideri went to her desk and held up the neatly typed and paper-clipped "looksist" commentary. She shook it at Casey. "Where did you ever come up with such a ridiculous and utterly false premise?" Then she turned to me. "And you, Rachel, wasting your writing skills on such trash."

I glared at Casey. *Oh, that rat.* She must have confessed my part in this too, after promising to take the secret to her grave. I felt like killing her. *Never* before had a teacher yelled at me.

Casey still wouldn't look at me. However, she faced Mrs. Desideri with her head held high. "Calling you a looksist is *not* a 'ridiculous and utterly false premise,' Mrs. Desideri. I have proof." Dramatically, she whipped my suggestion sheet from her notebook, snapped the folds out of it, and handed it to Mrs. Desideri.

With her forehead furrowed, Mrs. Desideri studied the sheet. After a minute, she looked up at Casey with a puzzled expression. "So what? What does this prove?"

Casey got up and pointed at Mrs. Desideri's "No—has bcs" comment.

"All that says is that I couldn't give Rachel the job she wanted because she has the best copywriting skills in the class."

Casey's already fair skin went absolutely ghostly. "*BCS* stands for best copywriting skills?"

Mrs. Desideri nodded. "Yes. I couldn't spare Rachel for that easy little weather job when she's the best writer we've got."

Embarrassed as I was, pride flooded through me.

"We thought *BCS* was your abbreviation for braces," Casey muttered.

"*You* thought," I shot back.

Mrs. Desideri was biting her lip very hard. I had a feeling she was struggling not to smile. Still, she shook a finger at me. "You *both* had a hand in this. And let me tell you something, if this were a *real* television station or newspaper and you were both *real* reporters, I'd fire you on the spot! And furthermore, I might even sue you for libel just as movie stars sue the *National Enquirer*! Because there are laws against this kind of thing. You forgot the number-one rule of journalism: Check your facts! And the number-two rule: Get both sides of the story!"

I felt so ashamed I was afraid I was going to cry. Casey looked pretty miserable too.

"All you had to do was ask me what that *BCS* meant," Mrs. Desideri continued, "then we could have avoided all this unpleasantness!"

"I'm sorry, Mrs. Desideri!" Casey wailed.

"Me too," I said, mortified.

Mrs. Desideri tore the commentary in two and tossed it into the wastebasket. "Next time you two pull a stunt like this, you'll be picking up trash on the school grounds after school for a solid month!"

That was no big threat to Casey. She probably already did that on her own anyway.

"It won't happen again," I said to Mrs. Desideri as she shooed us out the door. I turned to Casey: "It'll never even have the chance to happen again with you and me, Casey Chase! You just stay away from me!"

The good news was, the cough drops continued to work like a charm. All that day and the next, every time Glenn's baby blues turned in my direction, I just popped in a cough drop and soon was beaming at him as bright as a Christmas tree.

On Wednesday, the day Cherry Hill and I regularly went to the public library after school, I actually went one step further. I was in the new biographies section, looking at a book about Princess Di, when I glanced up and saw Glenn coming through the door. I popped a drop.

He veered over and stopped in front of me. "Hi, Rachel," he said.

I smiled . . . and even managed a muffled "Hi, Glenn" around the cough drop!

That encouraged him to go on to ask, "How are you?"

My brilliant response: "Fine." But it was a start.

He smiled back, then went across the room to sit down at the nearest empty table.

I nearly danced over to Cherry Hill. She was in her usual library spot. Sprawled across a beanbag chair in the children's section, she was flipping through the latest *Seventeen* magazine.

"Why so glum, chum?" she asked sarcastically.

"I've got a book about a princess and I feel like a queen!" I sang out.

The librarian, at her desk, looked up at me with a disapproving frown. "Shh!" she said.

For a few seconds I was mortified as every person in the entire building looked my way. Then I caught Glenn's eyes on me from across the room. He was grinning and holding a thumb up.

I felt my spirits soar and my cough drop still working. I smiled back at him. And then at the librarian.

CHAPTER SEVEN

Thursday morning, the whole class assembled at the dumpsters behind the cafeteria for the taping of Casey Chase's commentary. Thanks to the "looksist" fiasco, she was going to ad-lib on some other subject—no one but she and Mrs. Desideri knew what that subject was—and she'd asked for this strange location for the taping.

Janie, behind the video camera, gave Casey a count of three and then Casey launched right in: "Our writers couldn't come up with much in the way of significant news here at Kennedy Elementary"—I glared at her, but her eyes were on the camera—"so I say we at Kennedy should *create* some news. I have an idea of how we can do that . . . and help the environment at the same time."

A bunch of kids groaned and Mrs. Desideri gestured sharply for them to shut up. The last time Casey Chase had gone on a campaign to help the environment, she tried to make everyone in the class sign a pledge that they wouldn't ride their bikes for a solid month as a protest. It had something to do with the way rubber is manufactured.

Casey pretended not to hear the groans. "My idea is that we, as a school, start what's called a compost heap."

Everyone looked at each other blankly.

"Here's why," Casey said, pacing in front of the dumpsters as Janie followed her back and forth with the camera. "According to the Environmental Protection Agency, our city dumps are disappearing under mountains of people's lawn clippings and fallen leaves. In the summer and fall, something like fifty percent of the stuff brought to the dumps is that kind of yard waste."

She stopped and faced the camera. "What's so tragic about this is that when yard waste rots, it makes excellent fertilizer. People should be using it for that instead of just shipping it off to the dump where it isn't doing anything but taking up space. Since they're not, I say we help them do it. Once our compost heap has rotted into what's called humus, we'll throw a Wheelbarrow Saturday.

Anybody in the neighborhood can get a free wheelbarrow full of our rot to use as fertilizer in their yards."

Casey backed up till she was leaning against one of the dumpsters. "Here's my plan: I'm going to ask the company that makes these dumpsters to donate one for our compost heap. Then I'm going to ask the cafeteria staff to save all food scraps for the project. Now here's what *you* can do: Bring your lawn trimmings and dead leaves from home. We can use other organic wastes too. Stuff like onion skins, hair trimmings, eggshells, vegetable parings . . . even burnt toast."

"Can you imagine how that heap is gonna smell?" Brent Milsap said in a loud whisper. A couple of people silently made the finger-down-throat gesture in agreement.

"I'll be typing up a list of acceptable wastes and you can get a photocopy in Room Eleven," Casey said. "I'm also going to need volunteers to help me tend the compost heap. There'll be a sign-up sheet for that in Room Eleven. It doesn't matter what grade you're in. We need you!" She grinned at the camera, then made a slashing motion under her chin to indicate to Janie that she was finished.

Janie switched off the camera. Casey went over to where she'd laid her notebook down. "Those of you in our class who are interested in volunteering can do so right now," she called, ripping out a sheet of notebook paper and holding it up. Nobody moved toward her.

Mrs. Desideri clapped her hands. "Okay, class, let's head for the cafeteria." We were next going to film Betsy's story, "How the Cafeteria Staff Comes Up with a Menu."

Casey brushed past me and Cherry Hill with her empty sign-up sheet. I was still miffed at her because of the looksist commentary. "Evidently, rot is not hot," I said with a snicker.

Cherry Hill burst out laughing.

Casey whirled around. "Rachel, that is *brilliant*! We'll call it the Rot Is Hot project."

She rushed after Mrs. Desideri to tell her.

When we got to the cafeteria, Cherry Hill first taped an interview with Mrs. Del Casale, the cafeteria supervisor. Then the camera crew set up to shoot several trays of typical cafeteria food. The hilarious thing was that none of the food was cooked—it was still frozen solid since the staff didn't normally fire up the ovens till eleven o'clock. So there it was: a frozen hot dog sitting in a frozen bun, a solid block of macaroni and cheese, rock-hard cream-covered sliced carrots that would break your teeth. The funniest thing of all was that

Mrs. Del Casale herself admitted—off camera, of course—that our viewing audience would never be able to tell that the stuff wasn't cooked. It was so blah that it looked the same no matter what you did with it.

As Janie filmed the food, Cherry Hill practiced the voiceover that the editors would add later to the pictures. Betsy had written a lot of dry textbooky stuff about how the cafeteria staff strove to plan meals around the four food groups. Evidently, the staff hadn't joined the 1990s yet, because while, yes, all of the featured foods were members of the four groups, they were also crammed with cholesterol and saturated fat, and fiber was about as abundant as chocolate chips were in the cafeteria's so-called chocolate chip cookies.

I stood next to Janie and watched her videotaping the food. Cherry Hill stood next to me, engrossed in the script Betsy had written. Mrs. Desideri scurried by, trying to do ten things at once. "Oh, Rachel," she said over her shoulder, "a couple of the boys mentioned they had some story ideas for you."

Cherry Hill looked up at me. "Do you think Betsy would mind if I left out this part about how they make the cheddar cheese that goes into the macaroni and cheese? I mean, it's something that's done at the factory—not here at school. And this piece is running kind of long anyway."

"I'd better ask her," I said, my eyes scanning the cafeteria for Betsy. "That's a pretty major cut."

"Never mind," Cherry Hill said absently, returning to the script.

My eyes hit upon Glenn Vandever on the other side of the cafeteria. He had been talking with some of the other news editors, but when he caught my eye he headed my way, big smile.

I groped in my jacket pocket. Glenn was probably one of the boys who'd told Mrs. Desideri he had a story idea. A cough drop was definitely in order. But wait . . . my pocket felt funny . . . like it wasn't exactly in the right place.

Oh, no.

I looked down and confirmed my worst fear: I wasn't wearing *my* jean jacket. I had accidentally grabbed Cameron's out of the hall closet that morning.

Glenn was now halfway across the room, coming closer. My lips began to quiver. Panic! Panic! Come in Twitch Control! Twitch Control! I shoved my hand into Cameron's pocket. My fingers closed around a marble. It was pretty large but, in desperation, I popped it into my mouth and started sucking away. Clammy with relief, I aimed a wonderful smile at the approaching Glenn and started to take a breath to say *hi*.

And then I choked. I sucked that big, smooth marble back in my throat and I was helpless. I couldn't cough, I couldn't speak, I couldn't think what to do. I tried to draw in some air to cough with and only pulled the marble in more firmly.

Mrs. Desideri grabbed Glenn's arm as he walked past her. She said something to him. He was delayed temporarily.

I tried to breathe a bit more desperately. I daintily hit my chest with my fist. The marble wouldn't budge from my gullet.

Cherry Hill was still engrossed in her script. I pulled on her sleeve. I moved my mouth and pointed inside.

She turned to me and her mouth dropped open. For what seemed like an hour, she just stood there gaping at me as I frantically pointed down my throat. Finally, Cherry Hill screamed: "She's choking! She's choking!"

My trusty fellow news writer, Julie Kooda, in a panic, came running up with a glass of water and *doused* me with it, as if that would help! After that, I was choking *and* dripping. And then I felt myself getting lightheaded. The gray-speckled tiles on the floor were moving like waves. I sank to my knees.

I was jerked to my feet. Someone behind me put their arms around my waist and did the Heimlich maneuver, thrusting both fists into the space just below my rib cage and squeezing. The marble flew out of my mouth, clinked softly on the floor, and rolled under a table.

Gasping for air, I turned around to see who had saved my life. *It was Cherry Hill.*

We were immediately surrounded by kids. "Cherry Hill saved her!" someone shouted, and the crowd began to applaud wildly.

That's when Janie came out from behind her camera, grinning and waving. "I got the whole entire incident on videotape!" she shrieked.

The applause and cheers were deafening.

Mrs. Del Casale was fighting her way through the crowd. She came up to me and grabbed me by the shoulders. "What did you choke on, honey? It wasn't anything we fixed, was it? You didn't choke on cafeteria food, now right?" The kindly, concerned soul was obviously thinking *lawsuit.*

I regarded her coolly. (Well, as cool as one can be when one is still a little breathless and blue around the lips.) I was just about to scathingly reply that it was a cough drop when that little creep Benny McVie crawled out from under a table. "Here it is!" he shouted. "She choked on a *marble*!"

I am quite certain Benny McVie will not live much past the age of twenty thanks to all of the curses I have put on him since that day.

But it got even worse. Benny pointed at Glenn. "She was looking at you when she choked, Vandever!" he shouted gleefully. "I saw her! Glenn Vandever leaves women breathless!"

Glenn bit his lip. He was obviously trying to hide how flattered he was by that remark. "Are you okay, Rachel?" he asked.

I nodded and managed a weak smile. My lips didn't quiver a bit. Hey, Rach, I thought, now *there's* the solution for the quivering lips problem. All you have to do is almost choke to death every time you see Glenn Vandever coming! It was a funny thought, but instead of a laugh I produced a sob. I wanted my mother more than I ever had in my life. I was terrified I was about to start bawling like a baby.

Then Mrs. Desideri came up beside me. "You need to sit down, Rachel," she said into my ear. "I brought you a drink of water." She pushed me onto a nearby bench and put a paper cup into my hands. There was no ice in the water. I guess she didn't want to take any chances that I'd choke on that too. I drained the water. I began to feel a little better, both physically and mentally.

There was still a crowd of kids around Cherry Hill, slapping her on the back and high-fiving with her. She was bright red but loving the adoration, I could tell. She kept murmuring modest stuff like "Aw, anybody could've done that" and "Doesn't *everybody* know how to do the Heimlich?"

Meanwhile, Marina had sprung into action. As Porter Delay followed her around with a video camera, Marina was interviewing students about what they'd seen and their reactions. Some samples:

Jack Nguyen: "When she fell on the floor, I was sure she was a goner."

Leslie Chinaberry: "I have never in my life seen anybody's eyes bug out like Rachel's did."

Benny McVie: "At first I thought she had a cold and was just so congested she couldn't even get a cough out. But then she started doing this"—he made hideous faces like a terrified goldfish—"and that's when I knew there was more down there than just snot!"

Jenna Riebaugh: "We had the opportunity to learn the Heimlich maneuver in Girl Scouts as part of a badge, but I was never very interested so I just skipped it. Now I think I'll go home and look up how to do it! I mean, Cherry Hill actually saved somebody's life because she knew how!"

Eventually, Marina—with Julie Kooda, who was helping her come up with questions for the interviewees—got around to me. She thrust the microphone in my face.

"I just want to say how grateful I am to my best friend, Cherry Hill Summers," I said, and I meant it.

Julie whispered something in Marina's ear. Marina turned to me. "Why on earth did you have a marble in your mouth?" she asked.

I glared at Julie.

"Oh, wait a minute, that's it—we're out of videotape," Porter said, lowering the camera and sparing me from having to come up with some explanation for the marble.

"Why did you throw that water in my face?" I growled at Julie.

She shrugged and grinned sheepishly. "I guess I thought it might shock you so the thing in your throat would come up. I was only trying to help."

"Well, you didn't! If I hadn't been choking to death, I probably would have drowned!"

"Well, aren't you in a lousy mood!" Marina said. "Here we go and save your life and all you can do is complain! Talk about being ungrateful!"

"*We* did not save me," I said. "Cherry Hill did."

She ignored me and sailed over to congratulate Cherry Hill, who was being videotaped by Janie. The crowd parted to let Marina through. "Cherry Hill Summers!" Marina said, sticking her head close to Cherry Hill's and smiling prettily at the camera. "You truly are Rachel's hero for life!"

CHAPTER EIGHT

The next evening, Friday, my mom sawed through the nine toppings on our triple-thick Super Slob pizza and handed a piece to Cherry Hill and a piece to me. "The way I see it, Rachel, there's no way you can talk the other kids out of running that choking incident on *The Room 11 Video News*. I mean, you were the one who begged them to come up with ideas for news stories, remember? If that wasn't news, I don't know what is."

"Yeah. If I didn't know you better, I'd suspect you staged the thing just for the show," my dad said, picking up his own slice of pizza and digging in.

"Daddy, nobody but *nobody* would allow themselves to be filmed looking like Brandy barfing up a furball for the sake of a little school TV show," Tina said. She and Cameron roared with laughter.

"Shut up, Bettina," I said. She hated her real name.

"Oh, lighten up for a change, Rachel," she said. "Honestly, you complain about Casey Chase taking herself too seriously. . . ."

I ignored her. "I don't feel they have the right to run the story," I said to my mom and dad. "It's like . . . like an invasion of privacy."

My mom set the butcher knife down on the coffee table and came over to me. "But it *isn't* an invasion of privacy. You could say that if it had happened to you here at home. But it happened at school in front of your whole class."

"And in front of a camera no less," Tina said. "You sure know how to pick a place to pitch a fit, Sis."

"Shut *up,* Bettina," I said again. "I choked. I did not have a fit."

"It sounded like one to me, the way you described it."

"That's enough now, you two," my dad said.

Cherry Hill was just sitting there quietly, picking the mushrooms off her pizza and pretending to watch television. I guess modesty was keeping her out of the discussion. She was, after all, the star of the story in question.

"What did your teacher say, Rach, when you protested their using the story in the show?" my mom asked.

I hung my head. "I haven't said anything yet. I wanted to get your opinion first."

My dad cut himself another slice of pizza and settled back on the couch with it. "Isn't it too late to do anything? Isn't *The Room 11 Video News* supposed to go on the air on Monday?"

"Monday at nine A.M.," Cherry Hill finally piped up. "But the editors are editing the show this weekend at Glenn Vandever's house. He's the head editor."

"Well, you could call him," my mom said to me.

Oh, sure. Knowing me, the receiver would be shaking so hard in my hand I wouldn't be able to get my mouth close enough to say anything to him.

"I am not going to call Glenn Vandever," I said flatly.

"Then I guess the show must go on," my mom said.

"Why did you have my marble in your mouth in the first place?" Cameron asked.

By then I'd come up with a weak but at least plausible explanation. "I thought it was a cough drop," I said.

"What a brain surgeon," Cameron said. "Cough drops are half the size of that marble. Plus they're sticky and they're not round. They're more like lumpy footballs."

"I was concentrating on other things," I snapped.

"I guess," Cameron said. "Anyway, I want it back. It was my favorite marble. Where is it?"

Cherry Hill opened her mouth to speak.

"The janitor must have swept it up and thrown it away," I said quickly.

It was a lie, and Cherry Hill knew it. She knew as well as I that Benny McVie had kept it. But she didn't say anything. Which was nice, because I was never—repeat *never*—going to march up to that little creep and ask him to give the marble back. I was hoping that he'd just forget all about it and therefore stop teasing me about it and reminding everyone else that I, Rachel Harper, only four and one-half months shy of my twelfth birthday, did not choke on something sophisticated like a macadamia nut but on a *marble*. Oh, *très bébé. Très* horrible!

Before I went to bed that night, I threw the rest of my cough drops as hard as I could into the trash can in the bathroom. They made angry little bangs of protest. I told them to shut up.

Monday was a truly terrible day. It started with the nine o'clock broadcast of *The Room 11 Video News.*

"Our major news story today involves my co-anchor, Cherry Hill Summers," is how Marina began, smiling her little half-smile. What followed was the entire incident plus every single comment that was made afterward. The editors hadn't cut one thing. Not even Benny McVie's disgusting "snot" remark, which cracked up everyone in the class. I could hear the kids next door in Room 10 cracking up too, since they were also tuned in to the broadcast.

After that, my class began to discuss the incident excitedly, ignoring the other stories that followed plus Casey's commentary and David Jenks's weather report, in which he called the "marine layer" of clouds the *submarine* layer. It was like they hadn't been present when the choking actually occurred! I could just imagine what was going on in the other classrooms, where the kids were viewing the incident for the first time.

At recess, Cherry Hill was mobbed by congratulatory kids. I was mobbed by kids who wanted to know why I'd had a marble in my mouth in the first place.

After lunch that day, Mr. Snodgrass, the principal, called a special assembly in the auditorium to honor Cherry Hill "for her heroic deed." She was called up to the stage and everybody clapped like crazy as he placed this homemade gold medal job around her neck. It was just a circle cut out of yellow construction paper. On it was printed, in felt pen, CHERRY HILL SUMMERS—KENNEDY ELEMENTARY SCHOOL HERO. It was strung on a piece of black yarn. I had to bite my lip to keep from laughing when Cherry Hill came down from the stage wearing it. It looked exactly like the crude little Olympic gold medals we used to make for our Barbie dolls.

When we walked out of the auditorium and back to the classroom, I kept waiting for Cherry Hill to snatch the thing off and complain that "It reminds me of those amateurish-looking things we used to hang on Barbie and Barbette. *Très bébé!*" But she didn't. In fact, she wore it all day and kept fingering it, as if it really were an Olympic gold medal.

Later, when we were walking home from school, some kids in Mr. Farmer's sixth-grade class came up to admire Cherry Hill. She said "Doesn't everybody know how to do the Heimlich?" in her I'm-so-modest tone for about the three hundred thousandth time that day.

When the kids walked away, I turned to Cherry Hill. "Obviously, everyone *doesn't* know how to do the Heimlich maneuver or people wouldn't be making such a big deal about the fact that you do," I said as sweetly as I could.

Cherry Hill exploded. "Well, excuse me for breathing! Instead of complaining, you should be glad I'm not walking around with a swelled head. You know what I *could* be saying?" She put her nose in the air. "Yes, I *know* I'm terrific. And so does everyone else. Everyone, that is, except for my best friend, Rachel Harper. The same Rachel Harper, by the way, who only happens to still be living and breathing on this planet because of me."

Well, sure *she* wasn't going around saying stuff like that, but other people were. And I was sick of hearing it. "If you hadn't done it, Mrs. Desideri would have, or Mrs. Del Casale," I burst out, before I realized how horribly ungrateful it sounded. "I heard Mr. Snodgrass say that *all* of the teachers and staff know how to do the Heimlich."

"You could have been dead or severely brain damaged from lack of oxygen by the time either one of them got to you!" Cherry Hill said. "And the other thing is— Oh, forget it. I'm not going to waste my breath arguing about it." And she turned on her heel and stormed off the other way.

For a few seconds, I was speechless. We'd had arguments before, but never one where one of us actually walked away.

"Cherry Hill, wait!" I called after her. "I'm sorry! It's just that . . . I guess I'm tired of hearing you say the same things, that's all. I *do* appreciate what you did! I do!"

I know she heard me, but she didn't stop or turn around.

It was a miserable night. Cherry Hill didn't call me. Finally, I called her. Mrs. Summers said she was in the bathtub and would call me back, but she never did.

As I walked to school the next morning, I worried about what to do. Should I approach Cherry Hill on the playground before school? What if she snubbed me in front of everyone? That would be so embarrassing.

But when I got to school, Cherry Hill wasn't on the playground. I saw her in front of our classroom talking to Mrs. Desideri. Both of them motioned me over to them. Cherry Hill was jumping up and down with excitement.

"Guess what?" Cherry Hill said to me, as if nothing had happened the day before.

"The mother of Madeline Addams—she's a fourth-grader—is a secretary at Channel Nine,"

Mrs. Desideri said before I had a chance to guess what. "Evidently, Madeline told her mother about seeing the choking story on our news show. And her mother told someone who works on the Channel Nine *Eyewitness News*—"

"—And they want to run our videotape on the *Eyewitness News* tonight," Cherry Hill interrupted. "And get this, Rach—get this!—Dianna Duvall, the anchorwoman, wants to interview you and me on the air right after! Can you believe it?"

"When?" I squeaked.

"Tonight!" Cherry Hill and the teacher shouted together.

"I'll go call your mother at work and ask her if it's okay," Mrs. Desideri said. "Cherry Hill's mother has already given her blessing, and she's volunteered to drive the both of you to the station this evening." She hurried off.

Wait a minute! I wanted to shout after her. *You didn't ask* me *for my blessing!*

But I kept my mouth shut. The idea of being on live television in front of an audience of millions petrified me. My lips started quaking just imagining such a thing. On the other hand, because of this, Cherry Hill and I were best friends again. She had grabbed my hands and was dancing me around in a circle.

"I'm sorry about what I said yesterday," I finally

said after we stopped to catch our breath.

"It's okay, kiddo," Cherry Hill said. "I'll try to come up with some new responses to people so you don't die of boredom."

And she did, too. When a couple of fifth-graders stopped to talk about the accident, Cherry Hill said, "It's nothing Rachel wouldn't have done for me." I liked that. It made me sound more like a fairly intelligent and capable almost-twelve-year-old than like a dumb, helpless baby. I didn't care if she said it a hundred times that day (and she did!).

Before Cherry Hill and her mother came to pick me up to take me to the Channel 9 studios after school that day, I snuck into my parents' bathroom for a supply of cough drops for the ordeal that lay ahead. But I could find only one. I slipped it into my pocket.

At the studios, we were ushered into a waiting room. Mrs. Summers proceeded to apply about two pounds of blusher to Cherry Hill's cheeks. She looked like an overripe apple.

A man named Don—I think he said he was the floor director—came in a few minutes later and announced that they were ready for us. He took one look at Cherry Hill and came at her with a handkerchief. "She's wearing much too much makeup!" he said to Mrs. Summers. "She looks twenty-five!"

Mrs. Summers swatted the handkerchief away from Cherry Hill's face. "She's blonde and pale!" Mrs. Summers snapped. "She'll fade into the background without it."

Don sighed, stuffed the handkerchief back into his pocket, and motioned us to follow him down a long hall. No one had suggested makeup for my own naked face. I figured they wanted me to look as young as possible to add to the drama of the story. It annoyed me, but I was too scared about the upcoming live interview to say anything. In fact, I was so scared that I don't know how I managed to walk. I guess I was on automatic pilot. I was so scared that when I tried to put the cough drop into my mouth, I missed! It hit my cheek and flew onto the floor. I grabbed it and got it in right the second time.

But not without Don seeing me do it. "No gum chewing," he said sternly, shaking a finger at me.

I pushed the cough drop into one cheek with my tongue. "I'm not," I said. Rachel Chipmunk.

But he didn't seem to notice. He stopped us in front of some heavy doors. "Your tape is on right now," he said. "I'll show you where to sit and take you out as soon as your segment is finished. It gets pretty frantic in there."

We nodded and he led us through the doors into a big room blazing with lights where Dianna

Duvall sat at a long, skinny desk with the other anchor, Stan Malomar. The entire rest of the room was filled with wires, television cameras, and people running around wearing headphones. Dianna and Stan sat in front of this huge picture of the harbor filled with glistening white boats. The really hilarious thing was that until that moment, I had always assumed that they were sitting in front of a window and that the boats were the view from the window. Now I saw that if there really had been a window in the studio, the view would have been of the studio parking lot and the ugly, squat, gray building next door to it. I would have laughed out loud if I hadn't been so nervous.

Don kept making the *Shh!* gesture at us even though we hadn't made a peep since we entered the room. He pointed at a big television monitor. There I was, bug-eyed and choking to death. Don ushered Cherry Hill and me into two chairs set up next to Dianna's. Mrs. Summers pushed Cherry Hill into the one next to Dianna and I slid into the one on the end.

"Hi!" Dianna whispered. Her eyes were riveted on the monitor.

We waved hello, though my wave looked more like a karate chop.

They cut off the videotape right after Cherry Hill saves me. They didn't run any of the comments, including Benny McVie's "snot" one. Don, wearing earphones and crouching beside a camera, pointed at Dianna and she immediately put on a huge smile.

"Incredible footage, isn't it?" she said to the camera. "And I'm delighted to tell you that we have Cherry Hill Summers and Rachel Harper as our guests in the studio this evening. Cherry Hill, I can't begin to tell you how impressed I am."

"Thank you," Cherry Hill said, smiling. "Rachel would have done the same for me."

Then Dianna Duvall asked Cherry Hill where she'd learned to do the Heimlich maneuver. Cherry Hill launched into her story—the one about learning it in a Brownie troop four years ago and blah blah blah. The same story I'd heard forty-three times in the past five days. I didn't really listen because I was busy worrying about what Dianna was going to ask me. When she finally did—"How many seconds elapsed, Rachel, between the time you first started to choke and the time the object flew out?" (as if I'd been holding a stopwatch!)—Cherry Hill answered it for me, much to my relief.

The next thing I knew, Cherry Hill was grabbing me around the waist.

"Oof!" I said as Cherry Hill thrust her fists under

my rib cage. And that, as it turns out, was the only word I uttered on the Channel 9 *Eyewitness News*. Dianna said, "We'll be right back after this message," and Don rushed us off the set.

"Thanks," Dianna and Stan called after us absently. Each was busy looking into a hand mirror.

I was in no hurry to get home and face the teasing I knew there'd be. I could already hear Tina: "Today, Rachel Marie Harper made her sensational television debut: 'Oof!' "

But I had another surprise coming. When I got home, my dad was sitting at the kitchen table, drinking a cup of coffee and looking mighty grim and tight-lipped. Cameron was white-faced. Tina's eyes were red. And my mother was bawling like a baby.

She rushed up to me and gathered me in a bear hug. "Oh, honey, until we saw that videotape, we had no idea how close we were to losing you!"

Tina wiped her eyes with a tissue. "You really downplayed how seriously you were choking when you told us," she said, shaking an accusing finger at me.

My mom took a plate of food out of the oven and set a place for me at the kitchen table. Special occasion: I even got a linen napkin. Everybody else in the family—they'd already eaten—sat down at the table and stared at me as I ate. I felt like a zoo animal.

There was complete silence as I spooned stuff in, till my mom said, "Chew each bite eighteen times, Rachel. Remember that old rule of thumb?"

I finally got it. They were afraid I was going to choke again. "I'm not going to choke on pureed yams, I promise you!" I snapped.

That resulted in a fresh shower of tears from my mother. She got up and went to the kitchen phone.

"What's Cherry Hill's number?" she asked me. I told her. She dialed.

"Oh, Cherry Hill," she said after a minute, and the "Hill" was sort of a hiccup-sob. "How can I ever thank you for saving my baby's life? I will be eternally grateful to you, honey, and if there's anything anyone in the Harper family can do, you just name it and you've got it. Thank you, thank you, thank you again." She hung up.

"What'd Cherry Hill say?" Tina asked.

"Oh, she wasn't there. That was the answering machine."

My dad rolled his eyes. "I myself find it very hard to get emotional with an answering machine." But he squeezed my mom's hand as if to say, "I feel the same way."

CHAPTER NINE

"Rachel, look here!"

"Hey Rachel, over here!"

"Say cheese, darlin'!"

Without thinking, I smiled as three separate camera flashes went off in my face. The photographers, three men, were standing outside Room 11 before school the next morning. "Here comes one of 'em!" I'd heard someone shout as I rounded the corner.

Mrs. Desideri came out of the classroom with another man and two women. She introduced me to everyone. They were reporters and photographers from our three local newspapers—the *Courier,* the *Chronicle,* and the *Coast Times*—and had seen Cherry Hill and me on Channel 9 the night before.

"Let's try another shot, hon," the photographer for the *Courier* said to me. "You looked way too happy for a gal who nearly choked to death."

I had no trouble looking serious as he shot off a couple more frames. In fact, I actually glared at him, I was so annoyed. Was this story *ever* going to die?

The reporters gathered around and started barking questions at me—the same old questions even second- and third-graders had asked. What had I thought about when I was choking? *Why, I had been planning what to serve at my birthday party.* What was the first thing I'd said to Cherry Hill after she'd saved my life? *Hey, go easier on my ribs next time, willya, Cherry Hill?* Why had I had a marble in my mouth? *It had been in the macaroni and cheese, and now my parents were suing the cafeteria and the school district for eight million dollars.*

Actually, I gave the same old tired answers. Then one of the reporters asked a really stupid question: Was I grateful to Cherry Hill?

"Look," I said to her instead of answering the question, "isn't this sort of old news? Everybody probably already saw it on TV last night. And it happened almost a week ago!"

The reporter shook her head hard. "This kind of human interest story is timeless. Imagine: An eleven-year-old girl having the savvy to save her best friend's life. Most *adults* wouldn't have been able to do what she did!"

The male reporter nodded. "Wouldn't this make a great television movie?" he asked.

Was he *crazy*? "The whole thing only took about three minutes," I said. "How would you fill up the rest of the two hours? With commercials?"

I laughed, but they just looked at me as if *I* were crazy.

"There's Cherry Hall!" one of the photographers shouted, and the whole group abandoned me and raced toward Cherry Hill as she approached the classroom. I thought she'd be really annoyed about the guy getting her name wrong, but she was smiling as if she'd just won the Miss America pageant. And she sort of *looked* like Miss America too. She was wearing a brand-new black mohair sweater, a black- and pink-checkered mini skirt, and black pumps with skinny high heels.

Mr. Snodgrass came flying across the playground. "You people cannot interview or photograph these minors without permission from their parents!" he shouted.

"We'll get it, we'll get it," one of the reporters said, crowding up to Cherry Hill.

Mr. Snodgrass's face was fire-engine red with

anger. "And you people have no right to be on school grounds without permission!"

The photographer from the *Courier* waved him off. "We checked in at the front office. Lady there said it'd be fine, long as we signed in."

Mr. Snodgrass turned on his heel and stomped off toward the front office, shouting "Mis-sus Dale!"

Mrs. Desideri came up beside me. "I think Mr. Snodgrass wishes this whole thing would die down," she said.

You and me both, Mr. S.

"He's taking some heat from parents," Mrs. Desideri continued. "A couple of them called and want marbles and small balls banned from the school grounds."

Oh, brother, that's all I need, I thought, slapping my forehead. Then I'd *really* have the title Miss Popularity of Kennedy Elementary School all sewed up.

The bell rang. As the kids filed into class, they gawked at the reporters and photographers.

Mrs. Desideri gave Cherry Hill permission to stay out and talk to the newspaper people. None of them asked me to stick around, probably because I hadn't exactly been a wildly enthusiastic interviewee. Just as I was about to walk through the door of Room 11, the photographer from the *Courier* grabbed my arm and asked for my mom's phone number.

"Sorry, she's married," I said. I really did!

"Very funny," he said, but he laughed and I felt better. "I need to call your mother for permission to run your photo."

For an instant, I toyed with the idea of giving him a phony number. In the end, I told the truth. I'm just too much the timid type.

Cherry Hill didn't come in for nearly an hour. When she finally did, she was flushed and looked pretty. As she headed for her desk, she made a special point of waving and smiling at me.

We were in the middle of Social Studies, and for the last several days Mrs. Desideri had been devoting Social Studies to discussing "good journalism." I suspected that was because of the little stunt Casey and I had pulled.

"Did you spell your name and Rachel's for the reporters?" Mrs. Desideri asked Cherry Hill. "We do want them to be accurate." She aimed a meaningful look first at me, than at Casey.

"Yes, I did spell our names," Cherry Hill said. "Even though they didn't ask me to." There were several gasps from the class. Mrs. Desideri shook her head as if she couldn't believe it.

During recess, Cherry Hill pulled me off to a corner of the playground and pirouetted in her new clothes. "Gorgeous, huh?"

I nodded. "It's a great outfit."

"My mom was so thrilled about me being on TV that after we dropped you off last night, she took me shopping. You should see the other outfit I got. A really dynamite red jumpsuit."

"Red is definitely one of your colors," I said, remembering that Cherry Hill had had her colors done. The fashion advisor had told her she was a "summer." Cherry Hill had decided I was probably a "winter" and she listed the colors winters are supposed to look best in. But I never thought about it when my mom took me shopping. My only criteria for buying clothes were that they were comfortable, that they weren't so tight as to show how flat I was, and that they didn't have bows or puffed sleeves, which made me look eight years old.

"Can you believe it?" Cherry Hill was saying. "My mom's always crabbing about not having any money, and here she goes out and gets me *two* new outfits at Charlotte Russe. Wait'll she sees us in all three newspapers tomorrow. I'm gonna hit her up for a new pair of high tops."

"You ought to hit up *my* mom too, while you're

at it," I said. "Did you get her message?"

Cherry Hill laughed and nodded. "You know what we ought to do? You come over to my apartment this weekend and save me from drowning in the pool. Then we could get *you* all outfitted too." The idea cracked us both up. We laughed ourselves silly.

"That outfit is adorable. It's from Charlotte Russe, isn't it?"

We straightened up. Marina stood a few feet away, wearing her little half smile.

"I tried that outfit on at Charlotte Russe last weekend," Marina continued, "and I loved it. But my mom talked me out of getting it. We were looking for a dress to wear to my cousin's wedding. My mom wanted me to get something dressier."

"Don't you *love* Charlotte Russe?" Cherry Hill asked her.

"It's my favorite store," Marina said. "Did you see those silver-painted T-shirts?"

"*Yes.* They were so cool looking. You could put those with black leggings—"

"And silver socks," said Marina.

"And, like, a black and silver striped headband . . ."

I tuned them out. I had never even set foot in

Charlotte Russe because the smallest sizes they carried were juniors and you could have fit two and a half of me even in the tiniest junior size three.

When the bell rang, I trailed after Cherry Hill and Marina toward Room 11. Now they were talking about a black tube dress they'd both seen at Charlotte Russe. Snore. If dirty looks were swords, Marina would have keeled over dead, face first, right outside our classroom, and even Cherry Hill wouldn't have been able to save her.

The newspaper articles came out the next morning. The *Coast Times* and the *Chronicle* only ran pictures of Cherry Hill. There was a picture of me with the *Courier* article—one with my mouth in the shape of an *O,* as if I'd just shot a marble out of it. I looked ridiculous. I guess the photographer was getting back at me for my smart-alecky "she's married" remark. *Ha, ha, hon. I have the last laugh.*

Mrs. Desideri pinned the articles up on the bulletin board. She told Cherry Hill and me that she hoped we were writing down our experiences in our diaries. She wanted us to remember everything so we'd be able to update the story on the next edition of *The Room 11 Video News.* Oh, terrific. The story that wouldn't die. I told Mrs. Desideri I didn't keep a diary.

Speaking of the video news, that same day we

began meeting in our groups again in preparation for the second broadcast. Betsy, Julie, and I had no sooner arranged our chairs in a circle than Casey barged in. "I hope you guys are planning to cover the Rot Is Hot project in the next broadcast," she said.

I shrugged. Mrs. Desideri's crack about accuracy that morning had rekindled my anger at Casey.

"Well, you should," she said. "It's going very well, despite the lack of interest in it from this class." She tossed her hair with an injured air. "The dumpster company donated a big bin. A couple of the first-grade classes are making the compost heap their class project. And I've already started to receive bags of waste. Plus I've got a couple of volunteers from Mr. Farmer's room to help me."

"*Volunteers*?" I asked in my most sarcastic tone. I'd heard that the so-called volunteers were kids who'd gotten in trouble in class and were offered the choice between visiting the principal's office or helping with the compost project.

"Yes, volunteers!" Casey snapped.

I nodded at Betsy. "It's all yours."

"Come see my bin!" Casey said to Betsy, pulling her from her chair. Casey bounded out of the room. Betsy followed at a more sedate pace.

The next day, the phone rang from the time I got home from school till about midnight. It seems that the *Courier* article had been picked up by the Associated Press. That's a company that takes stories out of local newspapers and sends them to other newspapers all over the world. Anyway, every relative we have in the United States plus every friend my parents have ever made in the four different cities in which they've lived called to ask (1) if I was all right and (2) why I'd had a marble in my mouth.

The calls were annoying, but in a way I was glad we got them. They distracted me from the fact that this was the first Friday in months that Cherry Hill had turned me down when I asked her to spend the night. I missed her. She said she had to do something with her mom, but my mom felt Cherry Hill probably just needed a break from all the hoopla.

"A break? Give me a break," I said to my mom. "I bet *their* phone is ringing off the hook too." And I was right.

"My mom said the phone rang every three minutes," Cherry Hill said when I called her Saturday morning.

"Where were you?" I asked, hurt and suspicious.

"I . . . oh, I went to bed early. I was exhausted. You've got to admit last week was pretty hectic."

There was an uncomfortable silence. I was waiting for her to say more about going to bed early and I guess she was trying to come up with a way to change the subject.

"Guess what?" she finally said. "Before Marina moved here she lived only three miles away from where we did in New Jersey. In fact, she has a cousin who went to the same school I did."

"What brought that up?" I asked, more suspicious than ever. "When did she tell you that?"

"Oh . . . um . . . during one of the meetings when we were preparing to be the anchor kids. You know, at school."

I let it drop, although I wasn't sure I believed her.

More awkward silence.

"Want to come over this afternoon?" I asked. "If it's still raining, we can watch *The Little Mermaid*."

"*The Little Mermaid*? *Très bébé*," she said, yawning in my ear.

"Last year you said it was your favorite movie of all time," I said.

"That wasn't last year. That was a hundred years ago. Anyway, I can't come over. I'm busy. Have to go to the mall with my mom."

"Can I come?" Talk about acting desperate.

"Um, sorry, no," Cherry Hill said quickly.

"We're meeting this new guy my mom's dating for dinner afterward and we wouldn't be able to take you home."

I was about to suggest that my dad could pick me up at the mall when Cherry Hill said she had to go. She said "Bye" and hung up the phone before I could say "Bye" back.

I ended up watching *The Little Mermaid* by myself. And *I* thought it was every bit as good as ever.

CHAPTER TEN

If I had to pinpoint exactly when Cherry Hill started to turn into a snob, I would say it was the day, the following week, that she got the letter from André Beaulieu.

After the newspaper article appeared all over the country, people started to write to Cherry Hill "in care of Kennedy Elementary School, San Diego, CA." Some days, she'd get a whole bagful of mail from some second-grade class in a town like Klamath Falls, Oregon, or Wheeling, West Virginia. Sometimes during Social Studies, Mrs. Desideri would have all of us kids take turns reading these letters aloud to the class.

Snore. Was I the only person in the entire class who stopped finding it cute after the six hundred and fifty-second second-grader misspelled *Heimlich* as "Himlick"? Was I the only person in Room 11 who was getting slightly bored after hearing "What you did was awesome" for the four hundred and eleventh time? Apparently, yes. So during these read-aloud sessions, I clapped or said "Awwwwwww!" at all the appropriate places, just like everybody else.

The letter from André Beaulieu arrived on Wednesday. Mrs. Desideri chose to read this one aloud herself. And because she had studied French in college, she made an effort to correctly pronounce all of the French words sprinkled throughout the letter. It made André sound very poetic and romantic.

He described himself as "Paris born and bred, a high school senior newly arrived in Phoenix" where his parents had recently begun teaching French literature at an Arizona university. He praised Cherry Hill for her *charme* (charm, according to Mrs. Desideri) and her *bravoure* (bravery). He went on to say that he thought Cherry Hill had the "prettiness and presence of a movie star" and that if she ever found herself in Arizona he would love to meet her.

Here's what I thought: I thought he was just another phony Frenchman, like the one Cherry Hill had met at the Colorado dude ranch who had taught her the *très* dumb expression *très bébé*. I figured if he really was a French guy, he would have either written the entire letter in French or struggled to put the whole thing in English. Only an American would do something so obviously affected as use the French word *charme* when it was so close to the American word *charm*.

But the rest of the class was completely fooled—and floored—by the guy. After Mrs. Desideri finished the letter, there was a stunned silence until Roxie Campbell finally whispered, "He wants to *meet* you, Cherry Hill!"

Marina joined Cherry Hill and me on the way to lunch that day and the two of them talked nonstop about André Beaulieu. So nonstop that when Cherry Hill and I sat down in the cafeteria, Marina sat right down with us instead of adjourning to her own table, where she usually dined alone in regal splendor.

And that's when Cherry Hill made her first snobby move. Leslie and Kim came over to our table and started to sit down, like they usually did. "I'm sorry, but this is a private conversation," Cherry Hill said to them.

Both sets of eyebrows shot up, but Leslie and Kim didn't say anything. They just got up and moved to another table.

I aimed a look of surprise at Cherry Hill, but she

and Marina were too busy discussing André this and André that and blah blah blah to even notice. Soon they were talking about what Cherry Hill should wear when she met him, as if he'd actually set up a date! When fifteen minutes had passed and they were *still* talking about him, I decided I had to say something or next thing you know they'd be planning the Cherry Hill Summers/André Beaulieu wedding!

"What I'd like to know is how this André could know that you have *charme* just by seeing your photo in a newspaper," I said.

Cherry Hill and Marina regarded me silently for a minute. "Well, he could tell she's charming by the things she said in the article," Marina said.

"Just what are you getting at, Rachel?" Cherry Hill asked.

"That the guy is probably a phony," I said. "I bet you his real name is Andy Bolo, he's twelve years old, picks his nose in front of people, walks like a duck, and has never been out of Arizona in his entire life."

Now the old Cherry Hill would have cracked up at this, but the new Cherry Hill got all huffy. So did Marina.

"You know what, Cherry Hill?" she said. "I think someone around here is very jealous, that's what I think."

"I'm not jealous, I'm just being realistic," I said. "If he was really a debonair, eighteen-year-old French guy, he would have high school girls falling all over him and he wouldn't have time to write letters to sixth-graders."

You'd have thought I'd made some horribly insulting remark about Cherry Hill's *mother* by the way they reacted to that.

"Just ignore her," Marina said, and the two of them turned their backs on me—as much as you can turn your back on someone who's sitting on the same cafeteria bench—and continued to discuss the Great André.

I guess they felt that that was sufficient punishment, because after that lunch hour they went back to treating me normally. But nothing else returned to normal. Cherry Hill refused to go to the library with me that Wednesday afternoon, breaking a two-year-old tradition. "The moldy oldie smell in there has started to make me feel queasy," she explained. Then Marina began to eat lunch with us every day, as if, by allowing her to do so that one time, we had given her permission to make it a permanent thing. She started to hang out with us before school and during recess too. She probably would have even started walking home with us except that she lived in the opposite direction.

"Why do we have to spend so much time with

Marina?" I complained to Cherry Hill as we walked home one day. "She's the same old Marina you used to couldn't stand."

"Mm-hmm," Cherry Hill said. "But she's the one person who understands what it's like for me with all the media attention and so forth."

"Oh, I see. She was filmed saving someone's life with the Heimlich maneuver back in New Jersey, right?" I said sarcastically.

"No. But she understands anyway. She's just so much more sophisticated than the other kids." *Including you, Rachel.* She didn't say it, but she might as well have by the way she was looking at me.

Our daily walk home from school was getting to be the only time Cherry Hill and I were ever alone together anymore. In the week that followed, not once did she come over to my house after school. She said she had to go right home because her aunt DiDonna from L.A. was visiting for a few days. Aunt DiDonna was also Cherry Hill's reason for not spending the night at my house that Friday and for not being able to come over on Saturday or Sunday.

In the meantime, Cherry Hill got snobbier by the minute. If other kids tried to join us on the playground or at lunch, she or Marina would immediately say, "Sorry, but this is a *private* conversation." They'd say that even if we (or I should say *they*) were talking about something that wasn't private at all, like clothes at Charlotte Russe or videos they'd seen on MTV. Or they'd just simply walk away from anyone who dared to intrude. I would kind of drift after them, throwing an apologetic smile back at whoever they'd snubbed.

You'd think the kids would resent Cherry Hill for this kind of behavior. But no. They treated her like a star, just as they'd always treated Marina. They kept a respectful distance, but they followed her around and copied her every move. After the André Beaulieu letter, many kids even began to take up Cherry Hill's *très bébé* expression. I heard Leslie say it on the playground one day, and I pulled her aside. "*Très bébé* means 'very baby,'" I whispered.

"No, it doesn't," Leslie said indignantly. "It means 'how very babyish.' Cherry Hill says it does." As if Cherry Hill had the power to rewrite the French language!

Early the next week, as I choked down a fiber bar after school under my mom's watchful eye, she remarked that Cherry Hill hadn't come home with me in ages.

"She's been busy with relatives," I said.

"Oh, that's right," my mom said. "I saw her twice last week with her cousin—once at the movies and once at the mall."

"What cousin?" I asked.

The phone rang and my mom got up to answer it.

I sat there, puzzled, as she chatted with a friend. The only cousin Cherry Hill had was her aunt Molly's son Jeffrey, and he was only two years old.

"What'd this cousin look like?" I asked my mom when she got off the phone.

"Tall with long blond hair, like Cherry Hill."

Marina. I felt my face grow hot with anger.

"Did Cherry Hill tell you the girl was her cousin?" I asked my mom.

"Oh, no. I just assumed so. They didn't even see me. At the mall, they were busy trying on makeup at a cosmetic counter in Robinson's. And at the movies, they were way ahead of Dad and me in line." My mom peered at me with concern. "Why? Is that girl not her cousin?"

"Marina Dobbs is *not* Cherry Hill's cousin," I said bitterly.

"Oh. So that was Marina." My mom opened her mouth to say something else, then changed her mind. Instead she just reached over and patted my hand.

The next day, I had to hold my temper all day long until I could get Cherry Hill alone after school. While we spent recess and lunch with Marina, all I could do was glare at the two of them and fume silently about how sneaky they were. When did they make their plans—the plans that didn't include me? They had to be doing it by phone.

After school, we were barely through the school gates before I started yelling at Cherry Hill. "How could you? Going off and doing things with Marina instead of me is bad enough—but to cover it up too . . . to make up some flimsy story about your aunt DiDonna . . . oh, that makes me madder than anything!"

"What *are* you talking about?" Cherry Hill tried to look confused, but I knew her too well. It was an act. She had gone bright red. She knew exactly what I was talking about.

I told her about my mom having seen her with Marina.

"That was *not* Marina—it was Aunt DiDonna!" Cherry Hill said.

"Oh, quit it! My mom said the other girl had long blond hair. Your aunt has short brown hair."

Cherry Hill stamped her foot. "It was *too* my aunt. Ruthie's eyesight must be going."

"It is not," I said. "My mom has *perfect* eyesight!"

Cherry Hill stopped walking. But she didn't look at me. "Are you calling me a liar?" she asked in a deliberate, calm, and controlled voice.

I was about to shout "Yes!" when suddenly, out of nowhere, I had this crystal-clear vision: I saw myself approaching Cherry Hill and Marina on the playground. Cherry Hill turns to me and says, "Sorry, this is a *private* conversation." The vision was so vivid, so real, and so upsetting that for several seconds it hurt me to breathe.

I swallowed hard and turned to Cherry Hill. "No, I'm not. I'm sorry. I believe you," I said, although it was a lie.

"Okay, you're forgiven," she said lightly.

I had this strange, uncomfortable feeling that Cherry Hill had been hoping I *would* call her a liar. But why would she want me to do that? Maybe so she'd have an excuse to be mad at me. An excuse to not hang around with me anymore. Correction: To not let *me* hang around with *her*.

We walked on and I told her about a funny incident in one of my mom's classes the day before. A cat had wandered in, jumped up on a table in the front of the room, and cleaned his privates in full view of everyone.

Cherry Hill laughed politely. I was disappointed. In the old days, such a story would have sent her howling. But now she seemed to be thinking about something else. She just didn't seem to be there.

And that's how it was for the next several days. All day long, Cherry Hill and Marina would talk a mile a minute to each other while I stood silently by, occasionally interjecting a "Really?" or an "All right!" though neither of them seemed to notice. Then, on the way home, *I* would talk a mile a minute while Cherry Hill would glide along beside me, silent and lost in her own thoughts.

One day, right before we were going to split up into groups to make plans for the second edition of *The Room 11 Video News,* a monitor came in with a note calling Cherry Hill and me to the office.

My heart sank. It was probably another newspaper reporter wanting to do a story. There would be another flurry of publicity.

Actually, it was worse than that. Waiting for us in Mr. Snodgrass's office was a plump, enthusiastic little woman named Mrs. Snell. Mr. Snodgrass introduced her as an officer with the San Diego chapter of the American Red Cross.

"Someone in our office had a dandy idea," she said, bubbling over. "Why not have Cherry Hill

Summers and Rachel Harper tell their story and demonstrate the Heimlich maneuver at other elementary schools throughout the city?"

Oh, *dandy*.

Mrs. Snell went on to explain that, with our parents' permission, we would leave school for one hour a couple of times a week—preferably during art or one of our other "less important" subjects.

"Oh, I'd love to!" Cherry Hill said, clapping her hands.

As for me . . . no way! I'd have to stand up, petrified, no doubt with madly twitching lips, and do the whole awkward "oof!" routine in front of five hundred strange kids on a regular basis. Even the very idea sent my lips a-quivering.

"Come on, Rachel, say yes," Cherry Hill said, as if she could read my mind. Even her eyes pleaded with me.

And that's when it occurred to me that if I did agree to do it, we'd have to spend a lot more time together. We'd have to plan our presentation, practice it, critique our performance after each assembly, maybe even celebrate. The benefits certainly seemed to outweigh the disadvantages.

"Okay," I said, grinning.

Cherry Hill hugged me like a long-lost friend.

CHAPTER ELEVEN

Our first assembly was scheduled for the next Friday at Rolando Elementary. Every day, I bugged Cherry Hill about coming over to my house after school to prepare for it, and every day she brushed me off with "Don't worry—we have plenty of time." She said she had to go home right after school because she was on restriction for yelling at her mom.

"How long will you be on restriction?" I asked.

"A week," she said.

It seemed like pretty harsh punishment, especially coming from Mrs. Summers, who was the let's-have-a-talk type of parent, not the you're-restricted! kind. But Cherry Hill never told me exactly what she had yelled at her mother. Maybe, I thought, it was unforgivable.

If I had any suspicions that Cherry Hill was lying about being restricted, she was always at home after school when I called, and believe me, I always found a reason to call. Then I was suspicious that Marina might also be there, but if she was she was as silent as a floating tissue whenever I called.

By the Wednesday before our first assembly, I was having a full-blown panic attack. What on earth were we going to say for forty-five minutes in front of five hundred kids who'd be restlessly waiting for the final bell so that they could start the weekend?

In desperation, I called Cherry Hill's house that night, hoping her mother would answer the phone. She did.

"Mrs. Summers, Cherry Hill and I really need to spend some time after school tomorrow preparing for the assembly on Friday. I mean, I know she's on restriction—"

"Oh?" said Mrs. Summers.

I'll admit I have an overly suspicious mind, but that "Oh?" really did sound like it meant "She is?"

Nevertheless, I plunged on. "Look, we don't have to do it at my house or yours, Mrs. Summers," I said. "Cherry Hill and I could work on our speeches at the library instead. That way you'll know we're not goofing around or having fun."

"Well, sure, honey, Cherry Hill can go to the library after school with you tomorrow," Mrs. Summers said.

The next day, Cherry Hill was miffed. "It bugs me that you go and ask my mom like I'm a two-year-old or something," she said. "Can Cherry Hill come out and play?" she added in a baby voice.

"Well, I thought she'd need convincing by an impartial third party that she had to let you off restriction," I said.

It bugged *me* that when Marina told us—*told* us, not asked us—that she'd come along to the library, Cherry Hill didn't say, "Fine, but Rachel and I have a lot of work to do, okay?" So I said it.

Marina tossed her hair over her shoulder with a haughty flick of her wrist. "Fine. I have a lot of *homework* to do there. So I hope *you* won't bother *me,* Rachel!"

But she didn't do any homework. And Cherry Hill didn't work on our presentation. Instead, while I lugged heavy first-aid books from the reference section and waded through them for pertinent facts about the Heimlich maneuver, they sat at our table and whispered and giggled. First about some high school guy who was working at the book check-out counter. And then about somebody named Steve, who came in, picked up a sports magazine, and sat down two tables away. I vaguely remembered him from the sixth grade at Kennedy the year before.

"I love Steve's shirt," I heard Cherry Hill whisper to Marina.

"Then go tell him," Marina whispered back.

"You have *got* to be kidding!"

"No, I'm not. Do it."

"No way. Well . . . maybe I'll write him a note about it."

Cherry Hill reached over and grabbed the notebook I was making notes in. She tore out a piece of paper, wrote on it, then carefully folded it up.

"Will you pass this to the guy in the black shirt?" she whispered to a kid sitting at the table between ours and Steve's. The kid sailed the note onto the table in front of Steve. Steve picked it up.

"He's reading it!" Cherry Hill whispered excitedly.

I stole a quick look at Steve. His eyes were bright and he was smiling at Cherry Hill. "Thanks!" he mouthed to Cherry Hill, holding up the note. He looked really pleased.

"He likes you!" Marina whispered to Cherry Hill.

"You think so?" Cherry Hill asked, looking thrilled. "Well . . . I think I like him too!"

A minute later, Steve got up to leave. Evidently, he flashed another smile at Cherry Hill on the way out because Marina said, "He is obviously *crazy* about you."

I looked up from my book at Cherry Hill. "Do you think you could spend less time writing notes about guys' shirts and more time writing notes about the Heimlich maneuver?" *Ooh! Little Miss Goody Two Shoes!* But I couldn't help it. Not only was I doing all the work, they were acting like I wasn't even there.

"You want to know what I think, Rachel? I think preparing for this is a really stupid idea!" Cherry Hill's tone was so loud and angry that the librarian went "Shhh!"

"Look," I whispered, "doing these presentations was *your* idea, remember?"

"I know that," she whispered back. "What I meant was we're going to put every kid in the audience to sleep if we just stand up there and recite a lot of dry boring facts about when the Heimlich maneuver was invented and blah blah blah."

"I wasn't going to talk about *when* it was invented," I retorted. "But I did find some really interesting stuff about this Dr. Heimlich. I mean, he's invented some other really great things and—"

"I don't care how interesting it is," Cherry Hill

interrupted. "You wouldn't make it interesting. Let's face it, Rachel, you're not the world's greatest public speaker. Knowing you, you'd stand up there and read the whole thing in a dreary monotone, never once looking up."

Oh, that hurt! I felt my face flush red hot. What hurt most was that it was accurate. She had me down pat.

I must have looked horribly wounded, because she smiled gently. "I think we'll be much more interesting if we're spontaneous; if we just get up there and wing it," she said in a softer tone.

"I cannot wing it," I said. I knew if there was no prepared speech, I would just stand up there, petrified and silent. If I had a prepared speech . . . well, even if I *did* end up reading it, at least I'd be saying *something*.

"Yes, you can," Cherry Hill said. "Just follow my lead."

"You're not going to have to wing it for long anyway," Marina said. "The videotape alone is going to eat up ten or fifteen minutes. That is, if you run everybody's comments." She laughed. "Except for maybe that *très* disgusting snot one."

"We don't get to run the videotape," Cherry Hill told her.

It was the one saving grace of the entire plan.

Mrs. Snell had told us we couldn't run the video-tape because the kids sitting toward the back of the auditorium wouldn't be able to see the TV monitor and might cause a disruption. So while Cherry Hill could *say* I had looked like a cat barfing up a furball, the kids would have to rely on their own imaginations to picture it.

"But what we can do is take turns describing what happened," Cherry Hill said. "Then we'll demonstrate the maneuver. Then we'll simply open it up to questions. That'll kill the forty-five minutes, believe me."

And it turned out she was right. But I was right too. I was too petrified to say one word. Except for my "Oof!" of course, which was uttered by force. It's not that Cherry Hill didn't give me a chance to say anything. During the description of what happened, she'd say something, then pause and look at me to continue. Example:

"And then I felt someone clutch at my sleeve. I turned, and there was Rachel, waving frantically at me."

Pause. An encouraging look at me. Total silence.

Finally, she'd go on: "Rachel was moving her mouth and pointing down her throat. Then it dawned on me—she was choking to death!"

At the second assembly we did, Cherry Hill didn't wait for me to chime in, knowing that I wouldn't anyway. I just stood up there on stage next to her, my eyes on my shoes, while she animatedly described the scenario to the hushed audience. I have to hand it to her—Cherry Hill has a flair for the dramatic.

Meanwhile, I felt like her pet dog, heeling obediently by her side. After she finished her narrative, she'd say "Come on, Rachel! Let's show these people how to do the Heimlich maneuver" in the same tone one would say "Come on, Rover, roll over!"

"Arf, arf!" I felt like saying in response. Wouldn't that have been a cute and funny thing to do? But I was too petrified to make a sound. Except for "Oof!" of course.

Sometimes, during the question-and-answer period, someone would ask a question specifically of *me,* such as "What does it feel like when you're about to pass out?" That's when I would mutter something at my shoes. "It's kind of like the way a fever feels," I'd mumble with my lips quivering madly. Acting as if she were a United Nations translator, Cherry Hill would repeat my answer loudly and clearly into her mike: "She says it feels like it feels when you have a really high fever." Then she would go on: "You know how when you have a fever you feel really lightheaded and dizzy? Like you're half asleep? That's what it feels like."

By the end of our fourth appearance, this one at Robert Frost Elementary, I was furious at her for a little trick she had pulled at every assembly. She would always tell our story without mentioning what it was that I choked on. So always, *always* during the question-and-answer period, some kid would ask, "What did she choke on?" Cherry Hill would look at me, pause dramatically, and then almost whisper, "It was a *marble.*" There'd be a minute of stunned silence. And then the whole audience would rock with laughter and I would just die.

At the first three assemblies, I figured she'd simply forgotten to mention what it was I choked on during her spiel. But by the end of the fourth, I realized she was doing it on purpose. She was waiting for the laugh it got during the question-and-answer period. As the auditorium roared, she'd stand there smiling and shrugging in a very theatrical *You*-figure-it-out type of way. She loved it.

I made up my mind to complain. In the past couple of weeks, I'd made an effort to be super nice to her, to say nothing the least bit critical, hoping to keep on good terms with her. But it wasn't making any difference. She was spending less time with me than ever. Since we were winging it at the assemblies, we didn't need to get together to prepare for them. Neither did we spend any extra time together critiquing our performances, as I'd hoped we would. There was plenty of time to do that in Mrs. Snell's car on the way back to school from each assembly.

At any rate, those critiques were pretty much limited to Mrs. Snell saying, "You did a terrific job, Cherry Hill." Cherry Hill—whose head was getting bigger every day—wouldn't even thank Mrs. Snell for the praise. She would kind of toss her head as if to say, "Well, what did you expect?"

The fact of the matter was, her presentation was not always terrified. Sometimes, for example, she would change her story slightly in the same speech. She'd say that Janie had been filming the macaroni and cheese when I started to choke and later she'd say Janie had been filming the hot dog. Once, while answering a question, she mispronounced "Illinois" as "Ella-noys." Another time, she said "irregardless" when there is no such word—the correct word is *regardless*. Yes, maybe I *am* being too picky about these things, but remember, I'm the daughter of an English teacher. And right is right.

As for me, what was there to critique about my

performance? Except maybe that my "oof!" wasn't loud enough or something.

I still occasionally hung around with Cherry Hill and Marina before school, during recess, or at lunch, but they were too busy talking about *really important* things like whether the guy was saying "I'm not loud" or "I'm not allowed" in some song that they liked. More and more, I found myself spending my time with Leslie and Kim, although I felt kind of like a third wheel with them because they were best friends.

Cherry Hill didn't try anymore to deny that she was doing things with Marina after school and on weekends. She did, however, make excuses, and that gave me hope. Maybe this Marina thing was just a phase and Cherry Hill wanted us to stay best friends. For example, when she and Marina both happened to show up at a new Saturday gymnastics class the Y was starting, she tried to pass it off as a miraculous coincidence. And if her activities with Marina weren't some kind of coincidence, then they needed to do this or that together to prepare themselves for the second *Room 11 Video News* program. For example, Julie was writing a segment on what was hot in spring fashions—an idea that had come from Marina, not any of us news writers—and Cherry Hill said she and

Marina needed to go to the mall on Saturday afternoon to see if Julie's statements were correct.

Maybe the mall thing wasn't too much of a stretch, but their excuse for renting the Tom Cruise movie *Days of Thunder* to watch at Cherry Hill's one day after school *was*. Betsy and I were writing a funny segment about Kennedy teachers and the kinds of cars they drove. Cherry Hill told me with a straight face that the two anchor girls needed to study *Days of Thunder* in order to familiarize themselves with cars! Well, that movie is about *race* cars, for crying out loud! Give me a break.

The bottom line was: We did *nothing* together anymore except for those presentations. So what did I have to lose by criticizing her? Well, I suppose if she got mad enough she could turn the whole class against me. She had that kind of power now. The prospect made me feel sick to my stomach. I pictured myself sitting all alone at lunch, wearing a brave smile as I chewed on a sandwich and kids all around me laughed behind their hands at me or threw me dirty looks.

But then I weighed that unpleasant scenario against the embarrassment, the pain, the utter humiliation I suffered as I stood on stage in front of hundreds of kids and they laughed and hooted at me after the marble revelation. It wasn't much of a choice, but I decided the lonely lunch scenario would be easier on my crumbling ego than what I was enduring now.

"Look, why don't you just cut the drama and mention the marble right up front?" I blurted out in Mrs. Snell's car on the way back to school from our fifth assembly.

Cherry Hill turned to me, eyebrows raised in surprise. Then she shook her head hard. "We need it as an icebreaker," she said. "After the kids laugh they feel more comfortable about asking us questions."

She wasn't a bit angry after all. But I was boiling.

"But, Cherry Hill, it makes me look like—"

"Forget it, Rachel," she interrupted in a this-subject-is-closed tone. "It stays."

That was the day I started to hate Cherry Hill Summers.

CHAPTER TWELVE

But it was a secret hate. Advertising your hatred of the most popular girl in school would be social suicide. And anyway, she was still officially my best friend, wasn't she?

Sometimes it occurred to me that I really didn't hate Cherry Hill at all, or at least not all of the time. One recess on the playground, for example, I watched her and Marina laughing together and I felt this incredible stab of pure jealousy. You can't be jealous about someone you hate.

At home I spent a lot of time—the time I used to spend with Cherry Hill—just moping in my room. I even stopped joining the family for junk food and videos on Friday nights. I'd just take a piece of fried chicken or a Big Mac up to my room and read a book until it was time for bed.

One Friday evening, as I was on my way upstairs, I heard my mom say to my dad, "Rachel's going into *that* stage." I knew what she meant by "that stage." She was talking about how, at about twelve or so, Tina stopped wanting to hang out with the family. Tina once told me she'd rather spend the evening having her teeth drilled than be seen in public with her family.

But that wasn't the case with me at all. What I couldn't stand was the way they kept reminding me about Cherry Hill. My dumb brother kept asking "Where's Cherry Hill?" even though she hadn't come over in weeks. His rubbing it in like that—even if that's not what he meant to do—was hard enough to take. Even worse was the way my mom and dad never mentioned Cherry Hill's name and kept giving me these really sympathetic looks that made tears sting behind my eyes. They made me just want to hide away in my bedroom forever. Which was what I was doing.

One Tuesday night, my mom tapped on the door and came in. Tina was, as usual, in the closet on the phone. I was sitting in my rocking chair reading and my mom sat down across from me on the bed. For a few minutes, she described what she'd just learned from a television documentary about migraine headaches, something she got about once a month.

I pretended to listen, but secretly I was still sneaking in a few paragraphs of *Anne of Green Gables,* the book on my lap.

"Why don't you just sit down with Cherry Hill and tell her how much you resent the time she spends with Marina?" my mom asked suddenly.

I was so surprised by her sudden change of subject that my book fell off my lap and onto the floor.

"I mean," my mom continued, "maybe she just doesn't realize that what she's doing is making you miserable." Then she launched into a long story about how when she was a grad student at the university her best friend, Bea, had begun to invite an opinionated guy named Larry to eat lunch with them in the cafeteria.

"Larry really got on my nerves," my mom said. "Finally, I told Bea that if she continued to invite Larry to eat with us, I was going to stop eating with her and start eating with Debbie Farquar."

I laughed, but the last part of the laugh came out more like a sob. "You guys acted like ten-year-olds," I said.

My mom laughed too. "Here's the amazing part. It turned out that Bea couldn't stand Larry either. She had been inviting him to eat with us because she thought *I* liked him."

She peered at me, eyes narrowed with concern.

"Well, what about it? Could you talk to Cherry Hill? You might nicely hint that if she doesn't put a stop to this Marina nonsense, you're going to start hanging around more with . . . with . . . well, maybe that girl with the big teeth who came to your birthday party last year. What was her name?"

"Kim."

"Kim. Who knows? Cherry Hill might surprise you just like Bea surprised me. Maybe she puts up with this Marina because she thinks *you* like her."

I got up and went to the window and stared out at the cloudy, starless night. One of those huge spotlights was scanning the sky, probably to call attention to a new video store on El Cajon Boulevard.

"Mom, it's not the same situation as you guys had with that Larry," I finally said. "I'm positive Cherry Hill isn't hanging around with Marina for my sake. Marina never says a word to me."

I just stood there looking out the window with my back to my mom for the longest time. Finally, I heard her open my bedroom door to leave.

I whirled around. "Whatever happened to Larry?" I asked.

My mom chuckled. "He started to eat lunch with Debbie Farquar. In fact, he ended up marrying her. Today you know her as Debbie Chase."

My eyebrows shot up. "You mean the Larry you were talking about is Larry Chase? Your friend? Your office partner? Casey's father?"

She grinned. "Yep. He's mellowed out a lot since then."

When I arrived at school the next morning, I noticed a big crowd of little kids and their teacher, Miss Jennings, hovering around the doorway of Room 3, a first-grade classroom. Several of the kids were jumping up and down, trying to get a look through the windows. My news-writer radar went off, and I stopped to ask Miss Jennings what was going on.

"I think a sick or injured animal must have somehow wandered into the coatroom yesterday and died overnight," she said, buttoning up a little girl's sweater. "The smell coming from there is ghastly. Mr. Snodgrass called animal control and we've been evacuated."

My first instinct was to flee. At any moment, animal control might emerge with some neighborhood kid's pet Snoopy or Garfield and I did not want to barf up my Cheerios at the sight. In fact, the sight might set off a whole epidemic of barfed Cheerios. "Maybe we should move the kids elsewhere," I said to Miss Jennings.

But it was too late. An animal control officer burst out of the classroom, and I almost laughed out loud when I saw him. He was dressed in what looked like a space suit. He was wearing a big helmet and a plastic mask over his face. He probably feared the dead animal was contaminated with rabies or some other dread disease. He was carrying the dead thing in a brown paper bag.

"What is it?" several kids shouted, leaping around him in their excitement.

The officer opened the sack and pushed off his mask with a grin. "It's nothing but a bunch of old coffee grinds, two extremely moldy and partially eaten oranges, a big hairball, what looks like fingernail clippings, some gobs of a mayonnaise-like substance, and some eggshells." He held his nose. "P-U! Looks like some kid accidentally brought the sack of garbage to school instead of his lunch!"

The kids screamed with laughter. "It's not garbage!" one of them shouted. "It's for the compost heap!"

"The what?" asked the officer.

Miss Jennings took him aside to explain and I went off down the hall, grinning. Where were the video cameras when you needed them? The incident would have made a cute sidebar piece to Betsy's report about Casey's compost project. At least I could write it up and give the notes to Betsy.

Almost no one I knew was on the playground. Marina was there, standing by herself. Cherry Hill was nowhere in sight. I wasn't going to be a hypocrite and stand with Marina just for the sake of having someone to stand with. I sat down on a bench and made some notes about the animal control incident.

I looked up. Glenn Vandever had appeared over by the fence and was looking at a magazine with some other boys. I accidentally caught his eye, and he quickly looked away. I felt a little pang. He hadn't smiled at me since that fateful day in the cafeteria and I didn't expect him to ever smile at me again. I had this sneaking suspicion that he felt partially responsible for my choking and was scared that paying me any attention might trigger a repeat performance.

It got later and later. Still no Cherry Hill. Kids started to head for Room 11. Marina drifted by.

"Is Cherry Hill sick today?" I asked her.

She didn't even stop. "Mrs. Desideri whisked her off to the office the minute she got to school," Marina said, nose in the air.

I waited about thirty seconds and then followed Marina and the other kids into the classroom. The bell rang and we all sat down. Then the tardy bell rang. There was still no sign of Mrs. Desideri or Cherry Hill.

Kids started giggling and talking and throwing things. Benny McVie got up to write something stupid on the chalkboard. Before he could finish even one letter, however, Mrs. Desideri and Cherry Hill burst into the room, both of them beaming. Benny scurried back to his seat with a guilty look on his face. But Mrs. Desideri didn't even look his way.

"Guess what, people?" she called as she swept to the front of the room. "Cherry Hill Summers has been one of only ten children in America selected to receive a very, very prestigious award."

Don't tell me, I thought. Let me guess. She's being awarded for her gymnastic skill. She's being awarded for her clothes savvy. She's being awarded for her perfect handwriting.

"Because she saved Rachel Harper's life—"

Well, what a *surprise!*

"—Cherry Hill has been chosen to receive the Mack Marine Fighting Man Small Fry American Hero Award!"

For a minute, I was sure everyone would laugh. I mean, the boys in the class had outgrown the Mack Marine Fighting Man "action figure" several years earlier. And Mack Marine was sort of a joke. This doll—and it was a doll, even though boys would never call it that—was roughly the same size as Barbie and had no social life at all. All he ever did was throw grenades, shoot his rifle, and drive his tank. Not that he had the *clothes* for a social life anyway. He couldn't take Barbie on a date if his life depended on it. You had two choices of attire for Mack—his camouflage fighting clothes or his Marine uniform. One time Cameron had borrowed my Barbie sailboat and floated Mack around in it in the bathtub. Poor Mack had had to sail in his underwear. I had my Barbie go in there and shout that Mack ought to be arrested for indecent exposure!

But no one in Room 11 laughed about Mack Marine. Instead, they gave Cherry Hill a standing ovation.

"My mom and I get to go to New York City for a whole week—all expenses paid—to accept the award!" Cherry Hill burbled. For weeks she'd been acting so cool to everyone that this excited outburst surprised me.

A happy, enthusiastic Cherry Hill made a special point of asking me to eat lunch with her and Marina that day. I suppose she felt somewhat obligated to, since after all I was responsible for this latest bit of good fortune. But what did they talk about at lunch? Well, what else but what Cherry Hill was going to wear in New York. On the airplane. At the award ceremony. At Bloomingdale's. At the United Nations. At the Statue of Liberty. On the plane coming back.

"Oh, and you should tell the flight attendant on the plane that you're on your way to receive the Mack Marine Fighting Man Small Fry American Hero Award," Marina said to Cherry Hill. "They'll probably announce it on the plane's PA system and you might get to go up to the cockpit and meet the pilot."

I guess I was just fed up with everything, because I burst out, "Isn't it sort of humiliating to be called a 'small fry,' Cherry Hill? A small fry is someone who wears Pampers, or something you order at McDonald's."

Marina gave me a freezing look, but Cherry Hill laughed. "Something you order at McDonald's— that's pretty good, Rach." Apparently, she was in such a good mood that nothing could get under her skin.

But it did get under Marina's. "She's just jealous," Marina said to Cherry Hill.

Well, I *was* jealous. Cherry Hill was jetting off to New York, staying in some swank hotel, and sitting at the head table at some fancy shmancy formal banquet. Was that glamorous or what?

But my bad mood was due to more than jealousy. I had absolutely had it up to here (I am pointing at the top of my head) with the way this thing, instead of fading away into an interesting memory, just kept getting bigger and bigger.

We watched a really boring film about insects later that afternoon in class, and I tuned it out and started getting really depressed. I had this vision of Cherry Hill at twenty-five, *still* collecting awards and getting attention for saving my life a whopping thirteen years earlier. I saw her getting a medal from the President of the United States in the Rose Garden of the White House. I saw her accepting a plaque and a handshake from the Secretary General of the United Nations as three hundred interpreters translated the sentence "She saved Rachel Harper from choking to death on a marble" for three hundred ambassadors from around the world. Worst of all, I saw myself as a twenty-five-year-old career woman—a career woman, say, designing a new advertising campaign for the Ford Motor Company—and having the president of Ford ask me, "Why in the world did you have a marble in your mouth to begin with?"

I guess it was these daydreams—or should I call them daymares?—and the good-natured way Cherry Hill had laughed off my smart remark at lunch that made me keep making snide comments about the Mack Marine award to Cherry Hill all day. It was like I couldn't stop myself.

After school that day, Cherry Hill was actually walking home with me for the first time in weeks . . . even though it was only because Marina's mother had picked her up for a dentist appointment. Cherry Hill was rattling on and on about the way she wanted to get her hair cut for the trip when I blurted out, "How can you accept anything from a company whose product encourages six-year-old boys to love war?"

Once again, Cherry Hill just laughed. "Listen, for a trip to New York, I'd gladly come to school every day for a whole year wearing Mack Marine's full camouflage flak suit and that black stuff they rub on his face."

And once again, I decided she was just too thrilled about the whole thing to let anyone get her goat. But then, I wondered. Was it that? Or was it simply that she didn't care anymore what I thought?

To my surprise, when we got to my house she actually stopped, and I hadn't even asked her. I was really worried that my mom would fall all over her, shrieking, "Oh, Cherry Hill, sweetie, where have you been all these weeks?" But to my eternal gratitude, my mom was cool. She looked a little surprised as Cherry Hill breezed in behind me, but she just said "Hi, Cherry Hill" as calmly as if she'd seen her the day before.

Clothes, clothes, clothes. Clothes for the trip.

That was all Cherry Hill wanted to talk about, and my mom seemed really interested. At one point, she couldn't visualize a dress that Cherry Hill had her heart set on getting for the award ceremony.

"Wait a sec," my mom said, getting up. "I'll go get the Sears catalog. Maybe there's something similar in there."

"*Sears?*" Cherry Hill said in the same tone she'd say "The Salvation Army Thrift Store?" It stopped my mom in her tracks.

"What's the matter with Sears?" my mom asked. "*Très bébé?*"

"No, Ruthie," Cherry Hill said, shuddering. "*Très . . . un-chic!*"

In the old days, my mom used to dash out of the room before she started laughing at Cherry Hill's butchered French. But that day, she howled right in front of Cherry Hill.

I waited for Cherry Hill to explode with anger. But she laughed too. And finally, so did I.

CHAPTER THIRTEEN

The next day, on the way home from a choking assembly at Susan B. Anthony Elementary, I got the worst news of my life. Mrs. Snell and the American Red Cross expected me—and me alone—to do the choking assembly that was scheduled for the week Cherry Hill would be in New York.

"Couldn't you just postpone it for a week?" I asked in a squeaky, panicky voice.

"Rachel, all the arrangements have been made," Mrs. Snell said. "These things take weeks to set up!"

"Well, I just can't do it alone."

"You agreed to do these assemblies, Rachel, and it's only fair that you abide by that agreement," Mrs. Snell said.

Cherry Hill wasn't much help. "You can do it, Rach," she said absently, and continued to make a list of what to pack in her vanity for the trip.

Mrs. Snell took us home instead of back to school that day—it had been a late assembly—and I was in tears before I even made it through the front door. My mom caught me in her arms and I sobbed out the story.

She sighed when I finished. "Well, you'll just have to do it, that's all," she said.

That sent me into a new round of sobbing. "I won't do it! I just won't!" Then I had an idea. "What if I'm sick that day?"

My mom looked stern. She shook a finger in my face. "Oh, no, you don't! A Harper is not a quitter! A Harper is not a faker! I don't care if you're at death's door and I have to carry you onto the stage on a stretcher, you're giving that speech!"

"I can't!" I wailed.

"Yes, you can," she said. "I'll help you."

On Saturday my mom went to the library and came home with an armload of books about how to give a speech. She made me sit down at the kitchen table and we wrote out on paper what I would say. Then she had me turn those sentences into two- or three-word memory sparkers. For example, the sentence *The Heimlich maneuver squeezes all the air out of the chest, popping the stuck object out of the windpipe* became "squeezes/popping/windpipe." She had me transfer these memory sparkers onto three-by-five cards.

"What is the purpose of all this?" I grumbled.

She picked up the paper on which I'd written out my speech and tore it into a thousand pieces.

"This way you can't get up there and read the whole thing," she said, ignoring my shriek as she threw the pieces of speech into the trash.

Next, we adjourned to the family room with the how-to-give-a-speech books. My mom divided them between us.

She sprawled out on the couch with a fiber bar in her hand and a book on her chest. "What we're looking for are tricks to make you less nervous on stage," she said, munching away.

I pretended to look through one of the books, but I knew nothing would help. I was starting to nod off when my mom called, "Listen to this. 'Relax your hands as you're waiting to give your speech. Consciously make your hands go limp in your lap or let them hang loosely at your sides if you're standing. It's tough to remain tense when your hands aren't.' "

My mom sat up straight. "Let's try it."

At first I thought it was a dumb idea. But after I

tried it for a few minutes, I found that it really did work! I didn't feel drowsy as I had before—just calm, relaxed.

My mom agreed that it was an effective trick. "I feel as relaxed as I do when I first open my eyes in the morning," she said.

After that, I started paying attention to the book she'd assigned me. Before long, I found an intriguing tip. "Listen to this, Mom. 'One way to prevent your voice from shaking during a speech is to loosen it up beforehand. You can do this by shouting for a minute or two—preferably in your car on the way to your speaking location.' "

"That sounds like a good idea," my mom said.

I laughed. "But can you see me shouting in Mrs. Snell's car? DON'T MIND ME, MRS. SNELL! I'M JUST GETTING READY FOR MY SPEECH! BY THE WAY, I HATE YOUR GUTS!"

My mom cracked up, then got serious. "You can shout at *me* in my car. I'll drive you to the elementary school that day."

She did more than that. For days, she made me give my speech four or five times in a row, and she never yawned or otherwise let on that she'd already heard the thing thirty-five times.

The speech was never exactly the same. Sometimes I'd use slightly different words to describe how the Heimlich maneuver is performed or how I felt when nobody came to my aid right away. But my mom kept telling me that it was okay—I was still managing to get in all the pertinent information, and best of all, I was not reading it.

"Remember to find the friendly faces and speak directly to them," she coached. So I'd pretend that the mantel clock or our cat, Brandy, or a pillow on the couch was a face listening to me with rapt attention.

"What if I can't find a friendly face in the audience?" I whined at one point. "What if everyone is asleep?"

"You'll be able to find at least one friendly face," she said. "Mine."

"You're going to come?"

"Of course. What'd you think? That I'd sit out in the car waiting for you like your chauffeur? To the school, Jeeves. Veddy good."

"But what about your classes?"

"I'll get a substitute. This is too important to miss."

Every time I finished the speech, my mom—acting like the audience—would ask me one or two questions. Her questions were either very difficult—such as "What is the approximate diameter of the windpipe of a girl your size?"—or very embarrassing, like "Did you wet your pants as you were choking?"

If I giggled or complained about the questions, my mom would solemnly remind me that she wanted me to be prepared for *anything*. And then she'd refuse to go on until I answered the question, even if the answer was, "I really don't know."

By the end of the week, I felt . . . well, not *good* about the upcoming speech, but okay. On footage for the second *Room 11 Video News* program, in fact, I announced "I'll be doing the assembly by myself next Tuesday" as confidently as if I were Arsenio Hall. Of course, no one was there for the taping except Janie, who was running the video camera, and Marina, who was narrating the piece, which we'd entitled "Summers Saves Harper: The Sequel." But still, it was a start.

On Monday, I even found it in my heart to bring Cherry Hill a bon voyage present. I wrapped up the latest *Sassy* magazine, a new twenty-greatest-hits cassette tape (she was bringing her Walkman, according to several of her packing lists), and a giant Snickers bar (her favorite). I taped a big sign on the package—AIRPLANE SURVIVAL KIT. Cherry Hill seemed sincerely touched when she opened it. And I was the only person she hugged good-bye when her mom came to Room 11 at 10:30 to take her to the airport.

But on Tuesday morning, the day of my debut as a solo act, I was a wreck again. The assembly was to be held at Bernardo Center Elementary— clear across town—at ten o'clock, so instead of taking me to school, my mom took me out for breakfast at Denny's. My hands were shaking so bad I got water in my nose when I tried to take a drink.

"Relax your hands, remember?" my mom said, and when I did, I felt a little calmer.

As we ate—as I tried to eat, I should say—my mom wouldn't let me talk about the speech. If I tried to, she cut me off and changed the subject.

"Why can't we talk about the assembly?" I finally demanded.

"Because you don't want to talk about it, you want to fret about it," she said. "It would just make you more nervous than you already are." She put a forkful of pancakes in her mouth. Then another. "Mmm! These are great!"

I wouldn't know. I managed to eat only a tiny bite, and even that stuck like a furball in my cotton-dry throat. Luckily, my mom didn't force me to eat any of the shredded wheat cereal she ordered for dessert.

In the car on the way to the school, she finally allowed me to talk about the assembly, but only if I shouted, in order to loosen up my voice.

"I'M AFRAID THAT WHEN I SMILE MY LIPS WILL TWITCH UP AND DOWN LIKE A CAROUSEL HORSE!" I shouted.

"SO DON'T SMILE!" my mom shouted back. "NO ONE WILL EXPECT YOU TO SMILE! THIS IS A SERIOUS SUBJECT! YOU AL-MOST CHOKED TO DEATH!"

I remember sitting up on the stage next to Mrs. Snell before the assembly began. I remember the principal of the school, a Mrs. Demarest, intro-ducing me. I remember standing up and walking over to the microphone. I remember that as I walked my legs felt strange—tense and slow, kind of like I didn't have any knees. And I remember being surprised that the first sentence out of my mouth—"My class was producing a video news program, and we were videotaping a story in the cafeteria"—came out about six notes higher than my usual voice. I sounded like a cartoon squirrel. But evidently nobody else thought so, because nobody laughed. In fact, it was so quiet in there that you could have heard a marble roll down the aisle. They were listening! They were really inter-ested in what I had to say!

Most of the rest of the assembly was a blur, except for a couple of things. At one point, as I was retelling the choking incident, I got so involved in the story that I found—to my absolute horror—that I had sunk to my knees, just as I had when it had really happened. I caught myself just before I started to imitate my own gagging. This had never happened in all the times I practiced the speech for my mom, and for several terrible seconds I just knelt there, racking my brain for a graceful way out of the situation. Then, suddenly, the right words came to me. Sheepishly, I got to my feet and said, "I'll spare you the gagging part. If you're really curious, just picture the way your cat looks when she's trying to cough up a furball!" That's when it happened: They laughed! They laughed *with* me, not *at* me! Some people even clapped. I remember focusing on my mom's face among that sea of bobbing heads. She was just beaming. And discreetly flashing me the thumbs-up sign.

During the question-and-answer period it happened again: I, Rachel Harper, made an audience of five hundred people laugh. A little girl actually did ask me, "Did you wet your pants when you were choking?" I said a thousand silent thank-yous to my mom and then grinned and said, "No, but I almost did when I found out the whole incident had been filmed!" I tossed this off as casually as if

I'd just thought of it when actually it had come to me only after my mom had asked me the wet-your-pants question for the fourth time during our rehearsal week. Anyway, the audience loved it.

I'm not saying the speech went perfectly. Once, I accidentally skipped one of my cards and launched into the topics on the new card before I realized my mistake. I apologized and did some backtracking. Another time—during the question-and-answer period—a teacher in the audience asked me one of those textbooky questions that a kid would never ask: "How much has the number of fatal chokings in the United States decreased since the invention of the Heimlich maneuver?" I knew the answer but couldn't remember because I was getting more and more nervous as my time on the stage was drawing to a close.

Instead of being nice and simply giving the answer, Mrs. Snell—correction: Mrs. *Smell*—chided, "Now, Rachel, you *know* that."

"It has slipped my mind," I muttered. Fortunately, a kid was waving his hand, giving me an excuse to go on by saying, "You have a question?"

All in all, I'd say I did an acceptable job. An okay job. I did fine. My mom, of course, was full of words like *brilliant* and *fascinating* but we all know how mothers exaggerate.

Don't they?

CHAPTER FOURTEEN

Exactly one week later, in the middle of a Social Studies unit called "The Five W's of Good Journalism" (that's who, what, where, when, and why), Cherry Hill sailed into the room. I knew her plane had come in the night before, so she was obviously late in order to make a grand entrance. But I could understand that. I probably would have done the same thing.

Mrs. Desideri immediately dropped the journalism discussion. "Cherry Hill! Come up here and tell us all about your trip!"

Cherry Hill did just that, and she had stacks of pictures to show us. She'd hold one up, describe it, then send it down the aisles, admonishing everyone, "Touch only the edges!"

She had about eight million pictures of buildings, statues, and fronts of museums. I passed all those right on. I liked the pictures with the Small Fry American Heroes in them. There was a photo of all ten of them in front of a wall in Central Park. Nine of the kids were making funny faces or were in wacky positions; one little freckle-faced boy was standing on his head. Cherry Hill, however, sat serenely on the wall facing the camera, a knee tucked under her chin. Her new haircut was blowing a little in the wind. She looked like a professional model.

There was another picture featuring the freckle-faced boy at a hot-dog cart in the park. Cherry Hill told us his name was Derek and that the year before, when he was only seven years old, he had saved two strange kids who had fallen into a flooded river and were about to go over a thirty-foot waterfall. He'd jumped in, anchored himself with one arm to a rock, and, with the other, grabbed the kids as each floated by. If it hadn't been for Derek, they would have drowned or been dashed to death on the rocks below the waterfall. Anyway, Cherry Hill had shot the picture of Derek when he was on the other side of the hot-dog cart. He was so short that his head seemed to be coming out of the part of the cart where the hot dogs were stored. Derek was grinning, and it was really a cute picture. I told Cherry Hill it was a great shot at lunch in the cafeteria. She took about two seconds out of the monologue she was giving to Marina about the clothes she'd seen at Bloomingdale's to look at me and say, "Oh, thanks."

Yawning so hard that tears came to my eyes, I looked around the cafeteria for Leslie and Kim. I wished I'd eaten lunch with them. I caught Kim's eye and she waved but I stayed where I was. There was a sort of unspoken rule among kids at Kennedy that leaving one lunch crowd midway through the period to join another was the height of rudeness. Or a sign that a fight had occurred.

Then, I remembered something I needed to ask Cherry Hill. "Do you know where we're doing the school assembly tomorrow morning?" I interrupted her. "I don't want to leave here until the camera crew has finished shooting Betsy's story about Casey Chase's compost heap. The rot spot."

Cherry Hill turned away from Marina without so much as a smile at the last crack. "No sweat. We're going to Gage Elementary right over in San Carlos. It's five minutes from here, max."

"It's nice that we'll be doing the assembly *together* again," I said.

She nodded and turned away. "And this guy in

the lobby—he must have been, like, nineteen—well, he stared every single time I walked by," she said to Marina.

There. I'd given her an opening and she still hadn't asked me how my solo assembly had gone. That hurt terribly. Doing that assembly by myself had been the biggest, most monumental, scariest, bravest thing I had ever done and she had forgotten all about it. Or just didn't care.

"I want to do some of the talking at the assembly tomorrow," I blurted out.

Cherry Hill and Marina turned to me, their perfectly plucked left eyebrows arched up in slight surprise. "You do?" Cherry Hill said. "Okay, I'll let you answer most of the questions we get."

I shook my head. "No. I want to do at least part of the description of what happened."

"We'll see," Cherry Hill said curtly. It was exactly the same kind of dismissive this-subject-is-closed tone she'd used the time she'd refused to stop mentioning the marble as an icebreaker.

Well, yes, we *would* see, I vowed as the bell rang and we stood up to leave. What we would see is that I would no longer serve as the "icebreaker," Cherry Hill's polite term for *laughingstock*. That's what I had been during those assemblies with her . . . something for the kids to laugh at. Well, we didn't *need* a laughingstock. When I did the assembly by myself, I had proved that we could get our message across in an interesting, thoughtful, and even humorous manner without having to give the audience someone to laugh at. Namely, me.

The next morning, Betsy and I, Porter Delay and Annie Bos of the camera crew, and Devon Gonzalez, one of the *Video News* directors, met Casey Chase at her compost bin—which featured a huge hand-lettered sign reading ROT IS HOT!—to film the story. I hadn't read Betsy's script, so I was surprised to see her talking to a big man wearing overalls and standing next to a wheelbarrow. He reminded me of Willard Scott—the weather guy on the *Today Show*—only he had a beard.

Casey joined them, pointed at me, and the three came over.

"Professor Dugan, this is Rachel Harper," Casey said. "Her mom teaches at State too. She shares an office with my dad."

I shook his huge hand.

"Professor Dugan's in the agriculture department," Casey said. She went on to explain that she'd passed out fliers for "Wheelbarrow Saturday" in the neighborhood the week before and Professor Dugan was one of several people who'd shown up with his wheelbarrow. The camera crew had gotten it all on tape. And Professor Dugan had agreed to do some research on composting and come back today and talk about what he'd found out on camera.

Professor Dugan nodded toward the compost bin. "I fell in love with your humus," he said in a gruff voice.

Betsy giggled. "It's Casey's humus," she said, as if he'd said something like "I fell in love with your smile."

"Places, everyone!" shouted Devon, the director.

Casey wiggled into an enormous pair of rubber boots that went all the way to her hips. Then she kind of rolled herself over the top of the bin and landed inside, laughing. She threw some shovels full of humus into the professor's wheelbarrow. Porter Delay zoomed his camera in on the big man as he stooped next to the wheelbarrow, scooped out a handful of the muck, and held it to his nose. "Mmm! This is the best perfume on earth!" he said.

Betsy and I wrinkled our noses at each other, and Professor Dugan saw it.

"Come here, girls," he ordered. "Give it a try."

"E-yew!" Betsy squealed. I think she was remembering, as I was, that old egg shells and people's hair trimmings had been a part of the mix.

Still, the guy had a commanding presence, so we ventured forward.

Betsy took a sniff. "It's not bad," she said to the camera, her voice full of surprise.

And it wasn't. It had a kind of earthy, musky smell.

When Casey had filled his wheelbarrow about half full, the professor set off out the gate and down the street with Porter Delay filming him by walking backward in front of him and the rest of us tagging along behind him.

As Professor Dugan walked he talked about how plants convert the sun's energy into food for animals. Then the dead plant material can be collected and allowed to rot (or compost, the prettier term) into fertilizer that, when reapplied to the ground, essentially returns the sun's energy to the soil. "That's why composting is so important to food production," the professor said. "You could call the whole thing a 'cycle of light.'" I thought it was a lovely explanation of things and I felt sort of Earth Motherish just being around him.

His house was right around the corner and when we got there, Porter Delay spent a lot of time filming the professor shoveling the humus around his beautiful flower garden and among the tomatoes and cabbage plants in the vegetable patch outside his back door. His wife, large-boned and auburn-haired like her husband, came out of the house to help. On their knees, they worked side by side spreading and patting the new soil with tender loving care. You could tell this couple loved working the land as much as, say, I loved books.

Still, I couldn't resist a pun: "It's a dirty job, but somebody's gotta do it!" I said it so softly that the camera didn't pick it up, but the camera did catch both of the Dugans throwing back their heads and laughing heartily, their reddish hair glistening in the spring sunshine.

In Mrs. Snell's car on the way to the assembly the next day, I didn't say one word to Cherry Hill. Not that she noticed. She was busy telling Mrs. Snell about her New York trip.

A few minutes later, we were on stage. Holding the microphone, Cherry Hill launched into her usual account of the choking incident.

". . . As I read my script and silently rehearsed the lines I would soon say in front of the camera, I had no idea that Rachel, standing beside me, had begun to choke."

My cue. I leaned close to her and spoke into the microphone. "I had choked on a marble," I said, and my voice boomed throughout the auditorium.

"I was so busy and preoccupied with the story we were shooting that I mistook the marble for a cough drop."

There! I'd spoiled the little icebreaker she'd planned for later. A few people laughed, but that was it. Cherry Hill glanced at me in surprise. Then a look of annoyance flashed across her face and she moved away from me slightly, taking the microphone with her.

She went on with her narrative, and everything was cool for a minute or two. Then she said, "As Rachel gasped for breath, her eyes looked like Cookie Monster's—popped out and kind of googly and unfocused."

Now *that* was a new one.

The audience burst out laughing, and I felt a hot wave of red creep over my face and down my neck. I looked at Cherry Hill. She was grinning and basking in the response to her little joke . . . at my expense. So she was unprepared when I grabbed the microphone away from her.

"I felt myself losing consciousness, slipping away, dying," I said into the mike. "The gray-speckled tiles of the cafeteria floor spun crazily. But still Cherry Hill stood staring at me, frozen, her mouth hanging open like a freshly caught carp."

The audience absolutely roared with laughter. It

was Cherry Hill's turn to go red. Actually, she was so angry her color was closer to purple.

She reached for the microphone, but I curled my fingers around it, tight. She wrenched at it, but I held on. I had the advantage here. Sure, she was bigger and probably stronger overall, but she was an only child. She didn't have the toned-up super-strong hand muscles one gains from years of give-it-to-me fights with brothers and sisters.

Cherry Hill yanked, pulled, twisted. She bared her teeth with the effort. But I held my own.

"Give it back to me, you witch," she said, but the actual name she called me only *rhymes* with witch. Although she whispered it, the mike picked it up and broadcast it throughout the auditorium. There was a stunned silence, then some nervous laughter. Everybody in the audience started talking.

Mrs. Snell was suddenly between us. "Give me the mike immediately," she said.

I released my grip and Cherry Hill nearly fell on her behind, like a cartoon character when somebody on the other end of a tug-of-war suddenly lets go. The audience laughed. Cherry Hill's face turned an even more murderous purple.

Mrs. Snell took the microphone away from Cherry Hill and stood between us. She hollered for attention and then stamped her foot until there was just barely a rustle and a few muted conversations in the audience. In terse, short sentences, Mrs. Snell finished telling our story—she'd heard it often enough—and then asked for questions. There were six questions, run-of-the-mill stuff, and Mrs. Snell split the answers between us. She wouldn't allow either of us to touch the mike. She just held it in front of my mouth or Cherry Hill's, depending on who she thought should answer the question.

Both of us were pouting and subdued. I answered the questions directed at me in as few words as possible, and Cherry Hill did the same.

When it was all over, Mrs. Snell marched us off the stage. A kid walking by said, "The Adventures of Carp and Cookie Monster," and I glared at him, although later—much later—I remembered that and laughed.

On the way to the car, Mrs. Snell was still careful to walk between us, as if we might break into a catfight at any second. Who knows? Maybe we would've. I was angry enough to, that's for sure.

The three of us had just one further exchange of words.

"I'm not doing any more assemblies if I have to do them with her," Cherry Hill said.

"And I'm not doing any more assemblies if I have to do them with *her*," I said.

"You two aren't doing any more assemblies *period*," Mrs. Snell snapped.

CHAPTER FIFTEEN

Within hours, I became Rachel the Reject. Cherry Hill and Marina would have nothing more to do with me. They took great and obvious pains to stay as far away from me as possible. And although I'm certain neither one of them told the other kids what actually happened on stage at Gage Elementary—they didn't get chummy with the peasants—I did overhear Annie Bos telling Jessica Leeds in the bathroom that Cherry Hill and Marina considered me a hypocrite and a backstabber. And if the great Cherry Hill Summers and Marina Dobbs categorized me as scum, there definitely must be something wrong with me, right? So the other kids went out of their way to avoid me too.

At first I thought I was just being paranoid.

Surely at least a few of these kids still thought for themselves. Surely a few of them could see that I was the same old Rachel Harper I'd been two days ago, when they were all still smiling at me and saying "Hi, Rach" as we passed in the hall. But no. A couple of days after my fight with Cherry Hill, I tried a little experiment on the playground. No matter who I walked up to—just to stand next to, mind you, not talk to—they would quickly scurry away as if I had two-week-old b.o. or morning breath.

Cherry Hill and Marina were as snobby and as copied as ever, and things got even worse after Cherry Hill was in *People* magazine. It was just a big group picture—almost the same picture as the one she'd shown us of all the Small Fry American Heroes clowning on the wall. But you would have thought from the way she acted that they'd printed a photo spread on her alone.

Without even raising her hand first, she stood up in class on the day the magazine came out and announced, "From now on, you're all to call me Cher Summers."

Not *Cher* like "chair," but *Cher* like the actress. I thought it sounded phony and affected, but I guess I was the only one. Everywhere I went at school I overheard people talking about Cher Summers this and Cher Summers that. It was as if the name were music and people loved to hear themselves singing it.

One morning I watched Marina and Cherry Hill walking across the playground together and I muttered, "There go the beautiful people." I was just being sarcastic, but Annie Bos, who was standing beside me however briefly, said "Yes, they are" before she sidled away.

I was lonelier than I had ever been in my life. Even lonelier than when I'd been new at this school in third grade and didn't know anyone. At least then people hadn't gone out of their way to avoid me.

I spent every before-school period, every recess, every lunch hour all by myself. I found out pretty quick that I had to do something during all that time alone. I couldn't just sit there or stand there because I had nothing to look at. If I looked at people, they'd go out of their way to snub me by turning their backs or something. Reading a book was an option, but unless that book was absolutely spellbinding, I found myself looking up a lot. And getting snubbed.

The thing I finally found to do to fill the time was to write it all down—the whole story of what happened to me and Cherry Hill. I wrote constantly—sitting in the cafeteria, standing in line, walking out of the restroom. I kept hoping someone would jokingly ask "What are you writing, Rachel—a book?" so that I could answer "Actually, yes." But no one ever asked. So I just kept writing. One lunch hour, I wrote seven whole pages without looking up once. That was a record. My average was more like three pages a day. You can tell how long I was an outcast by how many pages you've read already. Weeks and weeks.

At home, though, I let my guard down and was a crabby, moody crybaby. One night at dinner, I spilled my milk and burst into tears although no one had yelled at me or even mentioned it. My mom and dad were always coming into my room in hopes of having a talk about what was bothering me, but all I ever told them was that Cherry Hill and I had had a fight and were no longer best friends. I didn't say anything about being Miss Social Outcast of Room 11. I was afraid that if my excitable mother found out about that, she would go to Mrs. Desideri and complain. If that happened, Mrs. Desideri might do something like force every member of the class to shake my hand and say that they were sorry. Such a prospect was so horrible that I burst into tears every time I thought about it.

Apparently, however, word did filter back to my parents about how dismal things were for me at school—probably via Cameron. I'm sure Cameron could've kicked himself three seconds after he spilled the story to my parents. Because guess what they made him do.

"Anybody sittin' here?"

I looked up from my notebook one day as a lunch sack slammed down on the cafeteria table across from me. Yep, it was Cameron.

He plopped down on the bench, hunched way down, and shoved a red apple into his mouth. His face was the same color as the apple.

I heard giggling from several tables. Oh, everybody was enjoying this. *Look at Rachel Harper—so lonely that she forces her little brother to eat with her.*

I smiled sweetly at Cameron. "I'm sure you're not sitting here of your own free will," I said to him under my breath. "I'm also sure you're well aware that there is one thing that looks worse than eating lunch alone, and that is eating lunch with one's brother."

"That's what I tried to tell Mom and Dad," he muttered.

"You can go now," I said. "I'll tell Mom and Dad we're eating together, that we're big buddy-chum-palsy-walsys."

Cameron nodded and got up, looking mighty relieved. He sauntered away.

"No offense!" I called after him.

"I know," he said, and I knew he knew. He understood how things worked at Kennedy.

I still felt all eyes on me, so I decided to get up and take a walk around school till the bell rang. I walked out the back door of the cafeteria and hadn't taken more than ten steps when someone called out, "Hi, Rach!"

I hadn't heard anyone say that for so long that I jumped, startled, and whirled around. Casey Chase was in her compost bin raking the stuff. That's when I realized Casey hadn't been avoiding me or snubbing me like the other kids were. The reason I hadn't noticed was because she was never where the rest of us kids were before school, at recess, or at lunch.

"Is this where you spend all your free time?" I asked her.

"Some of it," she said, raking away. "This stuff rots a lot faster if you water it and move it around every few days. Want to help?"

For a split second, to my surprise, I considered it. At least it would give me something to do to fill up the rest of the lunch hour. Then I caught sight of the hip-high rubber boots Casey was wearing. I pointed at my own pretty black suede ones. "Can't. Don't want to ruin these."

She nodded and I started to walk away.

"Hey. . . um . . . when did Mrs. Desideri say our class would get to preview the new *Video News?*" she called after me. "I forget."

"She said Thursday. The editors are still putting it together."

"Oh, that's right," Casey said. "I can't wait to see how the compost story turns out. We got some really good footage at the professor's house that day, don't you think?"

I nodded. She seemed kind of anxious to keep me there talking. That was all right with me, since I missed talking to people at school and at least Casey was acting fairly normal instead of her usual strident self. I leaned against the bin.

"Rachel?"

"Mm-hmm?"

"Rachel, did you . . . um . . . did you know that in the next ten minutes eight hundred acres of tropical rain forest will perish?"

I stifled a groan. She had to go and spoil it all by dragging in a cause.

"No, Casey, I'm sorry, I didn't know," I said over my shoulder, setting off. "But thanks for telling me."

That afternoon, after my orthodontist appointment, I walked through the front door and my mom said, "Hey, you're in *People* magazine." She held up the issue that contained the Small Fry American Heroes photo.

"That's old news," I said. My mom always read *People* weeks late because she only got them when the lady across the street traded us a bunch for a big stack of our *Time* magazines.

I grabbed a freshly baked fiber bar even without being ordered to and headed for the stairs. "Anyway, *I* wasn't in *People*," I said. "Cherry Hill was."

My mom shook her head and opened the magazine. "Your picture's not here, but they do mention you." She pointed to the caption under the photo. "See? 'Cherry Hill Summers saved a friend from choking.' That's you: 'a friend.' Now you'll always be able to tell people you were in *People*. I'll put it in your baby box."

Each of us kids had a baby box in which my mom had stashed kindergarten paintings, snapshots, and other memorabilia.

My mom made a move toward the family room where the baby boxes were stored in the closet. But I grabbed the magazine from her and hurled it across the kitchen toward the trash can. To my surprise, it sailed right through the trash can's trap door and landed inside. A perfect shot.

Instead of getting mad, my mom padded across the kitchen in her scruffies—her favorite slippers—and quietly retrieved the magazine. She brushed some coffee grinds off the back cover and tucked the magazine under her arm. "I hadn't finished reading it," she said.

For some reason, her calm reaction infuriated me and I burst into tears. I guess I wanted a fight. "How can you think I'd ever want to be reminded of such a disaster?" I said.

"It's just something that happened, Rachel," my mom said softly. "It wasn't a disaster. It would have been a disaster if she *hadn't* saved you."

I stamped my foot. "It was too a disaster! It ruined my friendship with Cherry Hill."

"Rachel, that's not—"

"It did!" I interrupted. "And it's all my fault. If I wasn't such a wimp, if I wasn't so disgustingly shy, I wouldn't have had that marble in my mouth in the first place!"

Her eyebrows went up. It was the first time I'd ever acknowledged to anyone that the marble hadn't been in my mouth by mistake. She looked curious but she didn't stop me to ask any questions. Not that I was stoppable.

"And if I wasn't so clumsy, if I wasn't as clumsy as a two-year-old, I wouldn't have choked! And then Cherry Hill and I would still be best friends and everything would be the same." I sat down at the table and buried my face in my arms.

I heard my mom sit down beside me. "In the first place, you're not as hopelessly shy as you think," she said. "A disgustingly shy wimp couldn't have gotten up alone in front of five hundred people and given such a dynamite presentation."

I raised my head. "That wasn't—"

She waved her hands. "Shut up and listen. It's my turn now. If you were as clumsy as a two-year-old, you couldn't have sailed that mag thirteen feet across the room and scored."

"Pure luck and you know it."

"And finally, you just can't seem to get it through that thick, stubborn skull of yours—that's one fault I'll readily admit you have—that your friendship with Cherry Hill was coming to a natural end anyway. The choking incident merely hastened it a bit because it made for some tense situations between you. But you two were already growing apart because of different interests."

"We were not."

"Rachel, you were. It was as clear as that window." She gestured at the window over the sink, which she always kept sparkling clean because she liked to watch the sunset through it. "You have nothing in common anymore except for memories."

"How can you say such a thing? We were best friends. We had everything in common."

My mom shook her head. "You like riding your bike and she prefers gymnastics, for example. She likes shopping, you like reading. She used to have to drag you to the mall and you had to drag her to the library."

"I did not drag her to the library!" I yelled. "She loved to go."

"No, she went only because she knew *you* wanted to. Are you forgetting the time I picked you guys up at the library and she accidentally left her library books in my car trunk? She didn't remember them till I found them a week later and you called her about them."

I shook my head so hard my hair made a slapping sound against my cheeks. "That was the week before Christmas, Mom. She had a lot of other things on her mind."

My mom just shook her head again.

"And anyway," I said, "she did not have to drag me to the mall. I liked to go."

"Only because you knew you'd end up having curly fries at the Food Court."

Oh, how could she be such a mind reader? It

made me even more furious. "Believe me, I'll like shopping a lot better when I don't have to shop in the stupid little girls' department anymore!" I shouted.

"But the point is, you don't like shopping *now*. And she does." She took me by the shoulders and forced me to look her in the eyes. "Rachel, your best friendship with Cherry Hill is over for good. And it's nobody's fault."

"You're wrong!" I shrieked, jumping up. I ran up the stairs, dived onto my bed, and wept.

It was a good twenty minutes before my anger at my mom cooled off enough that I could think rationally again. What had I meant when I said she was wrong? That she was wrong about its being nobody's fault? Yes, that's what I'd meant downstairs. But as I lay there and thought it over, I hoped somewhere deep inside me that my mom was wrong about the friendship being over for good too. I realized that no matter how angry Cherry Hill had made me, I still had a tiny glimmer of hope that eventually all of this would blow over, that Marina would miraculously bow out of the picture, and that Cherry Hill and I would go back to being best friends again. On that long afternoon that I spent crying and thinking, I finally even allowed myself to admit how terribly I missed her.

CHAPTER SIXTEEN

The next day, I worked on my book a little bit during lunch, then decided to kill the rest of the hour with another walk. I passed the compost bin. No Casey. Where did she spend her lunch hours, I wondered idly, when she wasn't composting? I walked past Room 11 and tried the door. Locked. She wasn't in there. Then I remembered somebody once saying that Casey spent her lunch hours in the school library, researching her various causes.

Since I had nothing better to do, I headed over that way and looked in the library window. Sure enough, there she was, sitting at a table all alone in the brightly lit but deserted little room. To my surprise, she wasn't copying facts out of *Consumer*

Reports or thumbing feverishly through an encyclopedia. She was holding a copy of *Seventeen*, of all things, and staring off into space. She was busy doing *nothing*. And she looked kind of wistful and lonely.

I was about to move on when she saw me. She turned a deep red as if I'd caught her sucking her thumb or something. I opened the door and went in.

For a minute I was tempted to rub it in a little by saying something like "*Seventeen*, Casey? I'm shocked. Seems a bit trivial for a person of your convictions." But then it occurred to me that I should *encourage* Casey when I saw her doing something normal like that. Maybe there was hope for her yet.

I nodded at the magazine. "I read my sister's. There's a really interesting article in that issue about how this entire high school class cheated on their final exam in a geometry class and got caught and expelled."

She flung the magazine down onto the table and tossed her head of springy curls. "I haven't read any of the articles. I couldn't get past the fact that the ads promote the idea that you have to be thin and tall and wear three layers of makeup or you're nothing. It's a facet of looksism that—"

"Oh, give it a rest, Casey," I broke in with a groan. "Did it ever occur to you that maybe you wouldn't have to spend lunch hour all by yourself if you weren't always shoving some righteous cause in people's faces?"

She flushed again and her eyes narrowed angrily.

I walked out, shutting the door behind me. I heard her yell. It was muffled, because all the windows in the library were closed, but I could swear she said, "And did it ever occur to you, Rachel, that maybe it's the other way around? Maybe I needed the causes because I was tired of being alone!"

I backed up and opened the door. She was standing there with a hurt look on her face, and I had the sudden urge to run over and give her a comforting hug. "What was that you said?" I asked her.

She shook her head, as if to shake off her feelings. "I said you're the last person who ought to be handing out popularity pointers!"

My charitable thoughts composted into nothing. I slammed the door and stomped off down the hall. She was hopeless.

That same afternoon, I got the reporter's break of a lifetime. I'd come up with a new system for walking home from school. Rather than face being taunted or snubbed by the other kids who were walking in my direction, I'd go to the library right after school and read a magazine for fifteen minutes. By that time, all the kids would be gone.

That afternoon, I made my way down the deserted corridors, down the school's front steps, and out onto the sidewalk. I heard a siren and saw a police car pulling over a familiar white convertible. Mr. Small, my fifth-grade teacher, was behind the wheel. I stood behind a tree, and I don't think either the police officer or the teacher saw me as they got out of their cars.

Mr. Small handed the officer his driver's license.

"You were doing forty in a school zone," the officer said.

"I . . . uh . . . didn't know there was a school here," Mr. Small muttered.

My jaw dropped. What a liar!

"Well, there's a sign posted right back there," the officer said, pointing. "The maximum speed limit here is twenty-five. And there's a reason for that. What if a child had suddenly darted across the street to catch up with his friends? What if a little girl came down that bike path and didn't stop or look both ways before sailing out into the street? Children don't have the common sense that adults have . . . or that adults are *supposed* to have!"

The officer was shaking a finger in Mr. Small's

face, and Mr. Small was staring down at his feet like an ashamed child. To see Mr. Small in the role of lecture*e* instead of lectur*er* . . . oh, this was rich! And on top of that, he had *lied*!

I had to restrain myself from clapping my hands with joy. Finally, here was a story that might overshadow—maybe even kill for good—the choking one. True, it was too late to get it into the second video news program, but there'd be plenty of time to write a dynamite story for the third one!

I forced myself to calm down and be a good reporter, as Mrs. Desideri was forever admonishing. I pulled out my notebook and wrote down the time—3:30 P.M.—plus the license numbers of both Mr. Small's car and the police car.

When I got home, I called the San Diego Police Department. The dispatcher looked up the police car license number. "That's Officer Tim Baer's car," she said. "I'll have him call you back."

That evening, when Tina and I were sitting on our beds doing our homework, my mom came in with eyebrows raised. "There's an Officer Baer of the San Diego Police Department on the phone for you," she said to me.

"Uh-oh, what'd you do this time, kid?" Tina said.

With quiet dignity, I took the phone and my

notebook into the closet and shut the door. To Officer Baer, I identified myself as a reporter for Kennedy's *Room 11 Video News* and asked him for the facts about the incident that had occurred in front of the school at 3:30 that afternoon.

"You mean about the guy I gave a ticket to?" he asked.

"Yes," I said.

"Well, Missy, I can only give you the facts that are a matter of public record. And those are that I issued a citation to one Bart Small for exceeding the speed limit in a school zone."

He waited for me to finish writing that down.

"Did he attempt to hide the fact that he's a teacher at that school?" I asked.

"He is? But he said he hadn't known there was a school on—" The officer broke off. "Now wait a minute, Missy. Don't quote me on that. *That's* not part of the public record."

"I won't quote you," I said. But I *could* say that he had confirmed that Mr. Small told a lie.

I thanked Officer Baer and hung up. Now all I needed to do was get the other side of the story. Oh, wouldn't Mrs. Desideri be proud? I'd have an eyewitness account (mine), that of the police officer, and that of the subject, Mr. Small. Talk about being thorough and accurate! I jumped on my bed and began making a list of questions to ask Mr. Small.

"What was that all about?" Tina asked.

"No comment," I said snootily. "It's confidential at this point."

CHAPTER SEVENTEEN

The TV screen went dark. Our preview of the second *Room 11 Video News* was over. Several people clapped. Benny McVie whistled. And then Casey Chase burst into tears.

There was an uncomfortable silence.

"What on earth is the matter with you?" Marina finally said.

I knew. And I'm sure Marina knew too. And probably most of the other kids.

Casey jumped to her feet and had the nerve to point at The Great Marina. Several people gasped. "You *know* what the matter is, Marina," Casey said. "You helped *them* edit the show." Now her finger flew toward the three video editors—including Glenn Vandever—who were sitting together the front. The three of them looked at their nails or out the window, anywhere but at Casey. Her accusing finger moved again. "And Cherry Hill Summers—you were in on the editing too! You and Marina—"

"It's *Cher*," Cherry Hill said, tossing her hair over her shoulder.

"Now, Casey—" Mrs. Desideri took a step toward her. But Casey waved the teacher away. She moved toward the editors.

"You gave the compost story about sixty-seven seconds tops," she said in that same choked and furious voice.

They *had* sliced it to nothing, and frankly I'd been shocked. They included some footage of the neighborhood people coming to get the humus on Wheelbarrow Saturday. But there was nothing of Professor Dugan, or his walk home pushing the wheelbarrow, or his talk in his gardens. There was no footage of the cheerful commentary about compost that Casey had given one day while standing in the middle of the muck. And there was no mention of my funny Animal Control story from Room 3. Instead, there was a brief voiceover by Marina that said almost nothing except that a few classes had adopted the compost pile as a class project and that neighborhood freeloaders, as

Marina termed them, had been the chief bene-
ficiaries.

Glenn cleared his throat. "Sorry, Casey, but we
just couldn't give it any more time. We just ran out
of time."

Casey snorted. "Don't give me that! You gave
the choking sequel more than ten minutes! I
clocked it."

"Oh, chill out, Chase," Marina said. "Even you
have to admit that Cher's trip to New York and all
the coverage she's gotten, including *People* magazine, Casey—*People* magazine!—is a lot more
interesting than a big pile of . . . manure."

A bunch of kids laughed.

It was such a stupid remark I just had to say
something. "It is *not* manure, Marina," I said,
looking her straight in the eye, "and if you people
had actually listened to what Professor Dugan and
Casey said on all the footage you so casually cut,
you would know that!"

Angry, how-dare-she looks flew at me from
every direction but nobody said anything. Talking
to me was forbidden by law, remember? Still, I
was proud of myself for speaking up instead of
cowering in class, as usual. I felt so *liberated*.

"I think everybody should try to . . . " Mrs.
Desideri started to say, then shook her head, folded

her arms across her chest, and leaned against her desk. She had obviously decided to let the parties involved solve this among themselves.

Casey sank into her chair and dropped her head into her hands. "I just can't believe you'd give such short shrift to something so worthwhile."

"What Cher did to save Rachel was worthwhile too, and certainly deserved to be covered," Annie Bos said loudly.

Casey jumped up again. "Yes, it *was* newsworthy . . . the day it happened. But everything that's happened since then—the *People* thing, New York, *Eyewitness News*—that's not news. It's just glitz! It's not keeping people informed. It's not helping them live their lives better. Aren't those the goals of a news broadcast that we all came up with during those Social Studies discussions?"

A couple of people nodded slightly.

"Now compare that with the composting story. That involves *lots* of Kennedy students, not just one. It's teaching people a better way. It's showing them an earthwise alternative to our being buried under tons and tons of garbage that is not only polluting our—"

She was drowned out by groans. *Oh, Casey, you had them. Then you had to go and over-Casey them.*

Casey clamped her mouth shut and stared out at

the class for a minute. "All right," she finally said sweetly, "if I can't convince you of the merits of the compost story, perhaps I can take the offensive and show you what's so wrong about trotting out the stupid choking incident and running off the mouth about it at every opportunity."

There were several gasps of protest.

"You're just jealous of—" Marina began.

"Let me finish!" Casey cut her off. She was really in her element—pacing, gesturing widely, corkscrew curls flying. "You people forget that there wasn't just a hero in that story, there was also a *victim*. Rachel Harper was a victim!"

My face flushed hot. I felt all eyes turn to me again and this time I had nowhere to look. Finally, I focused on a cuticle that desperately needed my attention.

"Yes, what happened to Rachel happened in public, so it was fair game in terms of being news when it happened," Casey continued. "But every time you guys drag the incident back into the spotlight, Rachel is victimized all over again! Embarrassed, humiliated, ashamed . . ."

My face was now about 198 degrees.

"What did she do to deserve this kind of punishment?" Casey continued. "All she did was make a simple mistake. She put a marble in her mouth and then choked on it—something any one of us could have done."

For some reason, no one dared to say, "I, for one, don't put marbles in my mouth!" I felt waves of appreciation flood over me for what Casey was doing, but I was also dying of embarrassment. Two little beads of sweat rolled down my cheeks.

"In Social Studies, we spent a lot of time talking about the legalities of journalism—like you can't print or broadcast the name of a kid who's committed a crime or how you can't take a picture of someone through the front window of her house without her knowledge. Yes, there are rules we *have* to follow by law. But what about the laws of humanity? The laws no one enforces but that everyone should try to live by? Things like being considerate, like respecting someone's privacy and feelings even if they screw up big time in public." She pointed at me. "Let her be, for crying out loud."

Casey flopped down in her chair and, like a final punctuation, the lunch bell rang.

Nobody moved for a long, silent minute. And then, Glenn and the other editors stood up and headed for the back of the classroom.

"I think you guys have some more work to do," Mrs. Desideri said to them, and they obviously agreed because what they had been headed for was the box of videotapes from which they'd put together the broadcast.

Everybody else got up and moved toward the door. Casey brushed past me.

"Thanks," I muttered.

"I didn't do it for *you*," she snapped, no doubt remembering our last exchange in the school library. "It was the principle of the thing."

And it was because of that principle that, on my way out the door, I dropped the notes from my interview with Officer Baer along with the questions I'd planned to ask Mr. Small into the wastebasket.

In the cafeteria, as I sat writing my book that day, I felt people's eyes on me. And I can't explain why, but those looks felt different. They weren't scornful. They were . . . apologetic. Still, nobody came over and spoke to me. After all, I was still under sentence of the Queens.

I glanced over at them and was shocked to find Cherry Hill's eyes on me too. The look in her eyes was . . . sad? Confused? I couldn't quite read her. Then, for a split-second, she opened her lips as if she was about to mouth something at me. But she turned away.

As far as she was concerned, nothing had changed between us.

And then, a few days later, a funny thing happened. It was early on a Friday evening and the doorbell rang. I threw the door open, fully expecting to see a guy Tina had been pining over for two months and who had promised to come by.

But there stood Cherry Hill and her mother. I struggled to keep my mouth from dropping open. Cherry Hill was hanging her head, and I could see that her ears were a brilliant red.

Her mother seemed flustered. "Rachel, honey, we need a favor," she said hurriedly, jangling her car keys. "I have to go out of town on a business emergency. Would it be all right if Cher spends the night with you?"

I was speechless. Cherry Hill wouldn't look at me.

"Of course you can spend the night, Cherry Hill," said my mom. She was standing behind me.

Mrs. Summers pushed Cherry Hill toward the door. "It's Cher now, Ruthie," Mrs. Summers said to my mom with an apologetic smile.

"Come on in, Cher," my mom said, taking Cherry Hill's overnight bag from her.

Mrs. Summers ran down the front walk, high heels clicking. My mom shut the front door. She took Cherry Hill's bag upstairs.

We were alone. There was a long, long minute of uncomfortable silence.

"What was your mom's business emergency?" I finally said.

"There was a big fire this afternoon at a hotel in L.A. that's one of her company's clients," Cherry Hill said. Her mom worked for a public relations agency.

More awkward silence.

"Why didn't your mom take you to Marina's?" I asked. I was dying to know. Had Cherry Hill and Marina had a fight? Was this the break I'd been waiting for? Was this the first step in reestablishing our best friendship?

Cherry Hill finally looked at me. "My mom says she doesn't know the Dobbses well enough yet."

I tried to keep the crushing disappointment I felt out of my voice. "Oh. Well, doesn't she know about us?"

"She knows we're not best friends anymore," Cherry Hill said. "But she doesn't know that—"

"You hate me?" I said.

"I don't hate you," Cherry Hill said.

Just then, the doorbell rang again. Tina flew past us to answer it. But it was just some kid selling candy. Pouting, Tina stomped back upstairs.

The interruption made for more tense silence.

"I don't hate you either," I said after a minute, suddenly eager to get us back on the subject of

188

our relationship. "I just don't understand why you started acting so different and everything because—"

She put a hand on my arm to stop me. "Look, we both know this is an awkward situation," she said kindly. "Let's just make the best of it, okay? Let's just try to be nice to each other and not fight." But I didn't want to fight. I wanted to *talk*. I started to explain that to Cherry Hill, but she was already galloping toward the kitchen. "What are you guys having tonight, Ruthie?" she called cheerfully. "Pizza Hut or Kentucky Fried?"

She sounded so much like her old Friday-night self that for a few minutes, even though I was annoyed that she'd cut me off, I felt hopeful again. Maybe things *were* going back to the way they used to be. But as the evening wore on, the hope inside me burned away like one of those skinny birthday cake candles.

We watched *Anne of Green Gables* on PBS. Since I had read the book for the first time only a few weeks earlier, I found the movie engrossing. Cherry Hill, on the other hand, was bored stiff. She yawned a lot and even let loose a loud impatient sigh when she thought the movie was over but it wasn't. She kept picking up and restlessly flipping through magazines before sailing them back onto the coffee table. All we had were a few copies of *Time* and *National Geographic* and they obviously did nothing for Cherry Hill. I caught her glancing at the mantel clock a hundred times. It was like she couldn't wait till it was tomorrow and she could go home and call up Marina and discuss really *important* stuff like whether Madonna's current hair color should be classified as platinum or as blond.

I was so annoyed that I began to watch the clock too, wishing it was time for bed.

If I had any hope that Cherry Hill and I would lie awake till two or three in the morning like we used to, whispering and giggling in the dark . . . well, throw a pail of water on that too.

"You're not planning to read and keep the light on, are you?" she asked through a yawn as we headed for my bedroom. "I'm exhausted and Marina and I have a gymnastics meet tomorrow."

"I'll just read for a few minutes," I said, digging through my bookcase for *Anne of Green Gables*. The movie had inspired me to read the book again.

I figured she was faking her tiredness as a reason not to talk, but she really did fall asleep practically the second her head hit the pillow.

I lay there and stared at her for a while as she slept. And that's when it first sank in that we really didn't have anything to talk about anyway. Oh, sure, we could rehash what had gone wrong with our friendship. Or the things we once did together. But what beyond that? I couldn't care less about Madonna; obviously, those were also her sentiments about Anne of Green Gables. I was as bored with her as she was with me. My mom was right: We *had* grown apart . . . too far apart to get back together.

In the end, Cherry Hill and I never discussed it. But, eerily, it was almost as if we had. Because when I accompanied her to the front door the next morning, she gave me a big hug. And when she pulled away, there were tears on her cheeks.

"Good-bye, Rach," she said.

"Good-bye, Cherry Hill," I said, and then I was crying too. Not because I couldn't accept that it was over. But because I finally could . . . and because that didn't make it any less sad.

CHAPTER EIGHTEEN

On Monday, on their way to the restroom, Cher and Marina passed the table where I was sitting alone in the cafeteria.

"Hi, Rachel!" Cher called loudly.

"Hi, Cher," I said.

It was the third such exchange we'd had that day. Cher was going out of her way to show everybody that she was no longer mad at me.

Gradually, the other kids started coming around. On Tuesday, they stopped purposely snubbing me. On Wednesday, they started saying hi to me again. And by Thursday, some of them were even making tentative let's-be-friends gestures. Leslie and Kim, for example, came over to talk to me in the cafeteria. And Lisa Feeney walked out to the playground with me at recess.

I spurned all of these attempts . . . well, as much as a person who is as nice and afraid of hurting people as I am can spurn. I just smiled and pretended to be busy doing something else (such as writing my book) or going someplace else (such as to the bathroom).

The truth was, these people left me cold. Cher, at least, had had a reason to be angry at me because of the fight we'd had on stage. But none of the other kids had. They hadn't even known why she had suddenly begun to consider me "a hypocrite and a backstabber." They hadn't, as Mrs. Desideri was constantly pounding into our brains, gotten both sides of the story. They had just blindly followed Cher's lead. They were like dumb sheep . . . and I prefer *people* as friends, thank you very much. *Really.* Surprising as it sounds—and it surprised me too—once I had the choice, I discovered that I'd rather be alone than hang out with people like that. I fully expected to go all the way to graduation without a real friend at Kennedy.

I suppose the perfect ending to this book of mine would be to say that no one ever mentioned the choking incident again and that I became best friends with Casey Chase. But hey, this is real life. It's true that the video editors did cut the choking sequel story to almost nothing in the second *Room*

11 Video News and that there were no further sequels in any of the news programs after that. But the incident came up in conversation both in class and outside of it every now and then. It became another bit of Kennedy Elementary lore, like the old story about how Mrs. Tarantino once nearly gave birth in the coat room of Room 2 and the one about how someone in 1979 had hung a pair of what were supposedly Mr. Snodgrass's underwear from the flagpole. But I can tell you that apparently Casey's remember-the-victim harangue had gotten through: Nobody ever mentioned the choking incident again in my presence without tacking on something like "It must have been a horrible experience for poor Rachel."

As for the possibility of a best friendship with Casey Chase . . . well, we did make some tentative moves toward getting closer. She invited me to sleep over one Saturday night; I invited her on a few of my Wednesday-afternoon trips to the library. I even allowed her to read parts of this book (she made me go back and put in all those technical descriptions of the compost process). But there were so many things we didn't see eye-to-eye on that we usually ended up arguing or silently pouting when we were together socially . . . and I got tired of that. So strike the best-friendship idea.

But we do work together. Quite a lot, in fact.

You see, in addition to my chief writer duties on the *Video News*, Mrs. Desideri assigned me and Casey to do what's called "The Harper-Chase Report" (doesn't that sound classy?) on all broadcasts. This is essentially a commentary that combines what the teacher calls my "hard-hitting writing" with Casey's "passion and inimitable delivery." Mrs. Desideri confessed she'd gotten the idea to combine our talents officially after she read our looksism piece—"Even though that was blatantly false," she hastened to add. Both Casey and I love doing "The Harper-Chase Report." She allows me to do most of the writing, and I give her most of the on-air time, although I do throw in an ad-libbed, low-key, and usually funny comment or two to tone things down a bit as I sit beside the violently gesturing, curl-bobbing Casey. The only problem we have is coming up with a topic on which we both agree. But we manage.

When she's not tending her compost pile, Casey even eats lunch with us in the cafeteria. Our only rule is that for the sake of our digestion, if Casey starts running off at the mouth or being too graphically gross about some cause, she has to shut up if we say, "Chill, Casey!" And the few times we've had to invoke the rule, she's obeyed it. So she's not hopeless after all.

You'll notice I used "us" and "our" and "we" in

the above paragraph. That's because, as it turns out, I didn't go all the way to graduation without a close friend at Kennedy. About three weeks after Cher stayed at my house, a new girl named Dani entered my life.

She rushed into the cafeteria at noon on her first day of school, slid about half a mile on some creamed corn someone had spilled, then tumbled another half mile. She finally landed at the foot of the bench I was sitting on.

"Dani McDade," she said from the floor. She put her hand up to shake mine. Instead, I pulled her to her feet.

"Are you okay?" I gasped.

Fortunately, she came out of the experience with nothing more than a bruised ego. Since that day, we've been best friends. Part of the reason for that, I have to be honest, is that Dani's a real klutz. Although she hasn't done anything quite as spectacular as that first slide, she has managed to get her head caught in our mailbox, to drop a bowling ball on her foot, and to shut a car door on *both* of her hands . . . all in one month! In other words, I think it's safe to say that if anyone is going to be doing any lifesaving in this friendship, it'll be *me* saving *her*.

It's not as though I don't still miss Cherry Hill

sometimes. The *old* Cherry Hill, I mean. Not Cher. Dani and I don't laugh together as much as I used to with C.H. Dani never tells jokes. Nor do we have two years' worth of fourth- and fifth-grade memories to rehash when we run out of other stuff to talk about. And Dani isn't allowed to sleep over. Ever. It's some sort of ironclad rule in her family.

But I'll say this about Dani. She always listens to my ideas and laughs at my jokes. She somehow manages to be right there whenever I'm upset about something, like a recent big fight between my parents and Tina about when she could start dating after which I was afraid they'd never speak to each other again. And in the end I think it's that, and not being available for the once-in-a-lifetime (if ever) occasion you need your life saved, that makes someone a friend . . . and *keeps* someone a friend. In the end, it's that kind of stuff— Oh, I'm sure you've heard the saying eight million times before, but really . . . *that's* what friends are for.

P.S. I taught Dani the Heimlich maneuver, just in case!

ABOUT THE AUTHOR

Jacqueline Shannon is a graduate of San Diego State University and has worked as a television reporter and a freelance writer for many magazines, including *Seventeen*. *I Hate My Hero* was inspired by a story she did on real-life young heroes.

Jacqueline Shannon's first novel, *Too Much T.J.*, won an honorable mention in the Second Annual Delacorte Press Prize for an Outstanding First Young Adult Novel. She has since written many books for young readers, among them *Faking It* and *Why Would Anyone Have a Crush on Horace Beemis?* She lives in San Diego, California.